Höv
M f g

S0-AXN-633

Jacoby greeted her with stony silence

"It won't start," Sarah said.

"You left the lights on. Didn't you?"

She started. She had turned the lights on in the blackness of the shed. She hung her head.

"Don't waste that look on me, you conniving Amazon! What do you want here?"

She met his blazing gaze with genuine astonishment. "Nothing. I told you—I got lost. I had an accident." Amazon!

"Sure. And I'm the tooth fairy. You want something, all right, and that's why you deliberately sabotaged our effort to get out of here. Who are you, and what do you want from me?"

Quinn Wilder, a Canadian writer, was born and raised in Calgary, but now lives in the Okanagan Valley away from the bustle of a city. She has had a variety of jobs, but her favorite pastime has always been writing. She graduated from the Southern Alberta Institute of Technology Journalism Arts program in 1979. Since then, she has free-lanced, and her list of credits includes magazine articles, educational material, scripts, speeches and so on. Her first novel became a Harlequin, marking a high point in her career. She enjoys skiing and horseback riding.

Books by Quinn Wilder

OUTLAW
HEART
Quinn Wilder

Harlequin Books

TORONTO • NEW YORK • LONDON
AMSTERDAM • PARIS • SYDNEY • HAMBURG
STOCKHOLM • ATHENS • TOKYO • MILAN
MADRID • WARSAW • BUDAPEST • AUCKLAND

Original hardcover edition published in 1990
by Mills & Boon Limited

ISBN 0-373-03191-2

Harlequin Romance first edition April 1992

OUTLAW HEART

CHAPTER ONE

'I'm all right,' Sarah Moore told herself. Her attempt at an intrepid tone did not even begin to take the edge off her panic. She most definitely was *not* all right. She was hanging upside down in her car, suspended by her seatbelt. Outside, the wind howled and shrieked, and sheets of rain slashed wrathfully at her car. The blackness was so intense that it seemed that night was an ominous blanket that had completely obliterated the landscape, swallowed mountains and forest whole, and seemed to be threatening to swallow her.

The blackness provided a bleak reminder that she was in the middle of nowhere. No—nowhere would have been almost comforting. She was in the middle of outlaw country.

It occurred to her that her car was very probably going to blow up. Cars that flipped over in the films always blew up. For a moment, the fear of being blown up conquered her fear of being lost and alone on a menacing night in an isolated wilderness. She frantically unsnapped her seatbelt, fell on her head with a bump, managed to find the door latch, and crawled out into the full fury of the storm. She scrambled to her feet, ran from the car, and then turned and looked back, bracing herself for the boom.

The boom did not come. Sarah felt irrationally irritated, and somewhat automatically filed the information in her mind under the heading 'Lies Hollywood Tells You'.

The rain soaked through her heavy sweater in seconds. Her thick hair became plastered to her head, and water ran down her face in rivulets.

Still she stood, paralysed, staring at the wreckage of her car, reliving the moment it had begun to slither out of control towards the steep ditch. She had been going too fast. She knew that. She had been exhausted, and yet, after weeks of driving, she had felt, finally, as if her goal must be getting close. Had pushed on relentlessly, despite the twisting, unpaved road, despite the storm, despite her weariness. A more experienced driver probably wouldn't be in this mess, she conceded woefully.

She shuddered, her cold reminding her that she should be doing something other than feeling sorry for herself. Find shelter, she ordered, pulling her eyes away from her crushed car, pulling her mind away from the thought that somehow she had survived all that twisted metal. Trying to pull her mind away from the foreboding thought that this was not a very auspicious beginning to a holiday.

A holiday? No, it was not a holiday. It was something quite different from that. A holiday was what she had told her mother and Nelson. But the fact that she found herself standing here in the middle of nowhere—correction, outlaw country—had nothing to do with the fun-filled days of frivolity and laughter and relaxation that one normally associated with a holiday.

No. It was a search. For Sarah Moore, too long lost in Sahara. Sahara...

'One-word names are so effective, dear,' her mother had said. 'Just look at Cher.'

Strange. Her father had known. Her father, a man she had only the most shadowy memory of. A memory that didn't fit all the accusations her mother had directed at him for years. A memory only recalled when she'd received that letter, forwarded to her through a law firm, which explained why it had reached her. Apparently there were hundreds of letters from him that hadn't.

'I see pictures of you lots, even though you're supposed to be the one taking them now,' the poignant, and very long letter had read. 'When you get tired of all this Sahara nonsense of your mother's, you come and see me. It's Sarah that I know and love. Sarah that I'll always love. I see her still in your eyes.'

And then she'd had the memory of sitting very still on a little stool, while her father, paintbrush and palette in hands, had grinned over his easel at her. A memory of being loved and loving. A memory that had appeared swiftly and had been gone just as swiftly, evading her efforts to run after it, to capture again that feeling...

'You come to outlaw country,' his letter had continued. 'It's hard to find. Supposed to be. That's how the people who live here like it, and want it. Good people, really, but outlaws, every dang one of us. Seeking refuge. Me from your mother. Others from other things. There was an underground newspaper in the sixties that started bringing people here. Draft dodgers then, different things now. Alimony dodgers, like me (ha! As if your mother needs alimony! Damned vulture. Ain't she shamed enough of feeding off you?). A few who are really on the run, from the law or from the other side of the law... Come, Sarah. Ain't no phone here, but we're pretty easygoing. Always room for one more.'

The letter had made her laugh and cry in turns. Her father's character had shone from it, and in that moment she had hated her mother for lying to her all these years, for thwarting his every attempt to contact her. Hated her, and yet, with the ambiguity so typical of her relationship with her mother, had wanted to protect her, too, against his allegation that Mother was a vulture. Even if she was.

That one hazy memory had been too fleeting and too flimsy to send her running to her father, however. She'd written to him, saying she'd been delighted to hear from him, and telling him, emphatically, that she would never be journeying to his home in the rugged and vast interior of British Columbia. Then, the very thought had made her shudder. Outcasts, fugitives, the great unwashed, living in shacks in a mountainous wilderness. It had sounded dreadful to her, and she hadn't cared how awesomely beautiful he had claimed it was.

But, then, her life had still been a life. She had kept his letter, a little treasure, in the back of her drawer, and for a reason she could not fathom she had also kept the somewhat comical map that had accompanied it. And, when her life had shattered like glass, she had not even thought about it. She had just known that she *must* go. Go to the only place in the world where Sarah Moore existed—her father's mind.

A very foolish and impulsive decision, she decided sourly now, hugging herself tight against the onslaught of rain. She shivered, and her eyes darted suspiciously into the shadows of the thick forest all around her. There was probably a band of murderous miscreants watching her right now. Or a band of bloodthirsty bears.

She was too cold to even be properly terrified. 'I am going to die tonight,' she moaned plaintively. Her words were consumed by the storm. The storm, which realistically posed more danger to her than wildlife—of either the human or fur-bearing variety. She tried to think when was the last time she had seen a light. A long, long time ago. By car. Not on foot. She would have to walk for days to return to that point. She doubted that her flimsy string sandals would carry her a mile, let alone further. Sturdier footwear was close at hand, but an inspection showed that the boot of her car would most likely never be opened again. She didn't feel the strength to walk, anyway. She felt exhausted and overwhelmed by her fear and her predicament.

She squinted half-heartedly at the ragged fringe of trees that bordered the road. She supposed she could go and sit under a bush, out of the rain. Entertain herself by picturing what the headlines would read when they found her body. By picturing her mother's reaction—and Nelson's. It gave her a rather morbid sense of satisfaction.

The forest was wet and dark and creepy. Her search for a little haven of dryness proved futile. With a sigh of self-indulgent despair, she sat down in the mud and wept.

And then she saw the light. At first it seemed like a mirage, there one second, gone the next. But, no, it was there. It really was there, the flickering quality caused by the shifting shapes of the wind-blown trees between them. Hope caused her heart to beat painfully. She wasn't going to die! And she *had* been following that dratted scrawl of a map so carefully. Could it even be her father's house?

She got up and ran through the trees, over the uneven and slippery ground, heedless of the tree branches that sprang out of the night to whip her face, heedless of the roots that reached out around her feet, tumbling her to the ground again and again.

It was only when she was actually there, when the grey outline of a building loomed up out of the night, that she stopped, suddenly uncertain and wary.

Even in the poor light she could tell it was a ramshackle place, weather-beaten and leaning. It reminded her of pictures she had seen of hillbilly cabins. No, that wasn't quite it. It was more like a place out of an old cowboy film. The kind of place where killer train-robbers sought refuge. That was exactly it. Hope faded and fear returned. She stood in the shadows, shivering uncontrollably, yet waiting.

Nothing happened. She could not hear the sound of drunken brawling. Guns were not going off. People were not staggering out of the doors. Silently, she moved closer. She could take a tiny peek in that one lit window.

She sidled up to the cabin, praying that she would see an old lady sitting in a rocking-chair, having tea, with a cat on her lap. Or her father, busy at a canvas. Cautiously, having to stretch to her full height of five feet eleven and a half inches to have her eyes level with the window, she peeped in.

The light went out so abruptly she nearly fell over, and then cowered, motionless, flattened against the rough exterior wall. Had she been spotted? She waited for what seemed to be forever. No one pounded out of the cabin in search of the intruder. She became aware that she was very, very cold. And that her caution bordered on the ridiculous. She could see that a light had been turned on in a different part of the cabin. She crept around the front of the building on silent feet, hesitated, and then went up the rickety stairs of a slanting porch.

There were two windows, one on either side of the stairs. The light shone brilliantly from one, more diluted from the other. She peeped in the one less lit. She could make out the shadows of furniture: a bookcase, a pot-bellied stove. The bookcase reassured her. It seemed so . . . so civilised. Her eyes returned to the stove. She licked her lips with yearning. She could see the red glow of a fire burning within it. She imagined the warmth that must be radiating from that stove.

Through a narrow doorway, the light shone brighter. She craned her neck and pressed her nose into the window. A kitchen. She could see a table top. A fridge. A bowl of apples. That settled it! Bandits did not read books and they did not eat apples. They ate . . . they ate chewing tobacco!

Sarah did a quick inventory of all that was in her range of vision. All right. It wasn't likely to be featured in *Better Homes and Gardens*. But it didn't look menacing, either. She had an impression of neatness and order.

The wind howled and the thunder cracked. She took a deep breath, and, stuffing away the remnants of her fear, walked boldly up to the door. She rapped smartly on it. The door must have been solid wood, because the sound of her knock was pathetically small against the raging storm. She waited politely. No one answered her summons. And her pretence at bold composure was not going to carry so far as to allow her to try the door and walk in, calling, 'Yoo-hoo.' Out of the corner of her eye, she saw something. She turned to see a large, round, ragged-edge saw blade hanging from the eaves of the porch roof. A backwoods doorbell, she deduced with relief. She picked up the mallet that hung on a rusting chain beside it, and hit the saw blade with all her strength.

The shock of the blow trembled down her arms, and the sound shattered the night, rising above the storm and reverberating for long moments after she had actually thwacked the saw.

Another sound shattered the night. A scream. A human scream followed by the crash of breaking glass. She whirled and looked at the cabin with dumb panic. So, *they* were in there after all! Fighting, crazed on hootch, breaking the dishes. She was about to bolt back down the steps and into the relative sanctuary of the night, when it dawned on her that the night was now eerily quiet, save for the storm.

With the tiny morsel of courage she had left, she tiptoed over to the other lit window and peered in. A crumpled male form lay on the floor, surrounded by broken dishes, scattered books, an overturned chair. She shrank back into the shadows, watching, waiting for his assailant to return. Nothing happened—except that he cursed, a loud and pained blue streak. The words should have been enough to prove that he was indeed a rough-spoken and dangerous man, should have been quite enough to send her back into the night.

Instead, they reassured her in the oddest way. It was a human being in there, lying on that floor feeling pain. Flesh and blood. Known now, somehow, and less threatening than the shadowy images of her overwrought imagination.

Her heart hammering in her throat, she went and tried the door. It creaked open under the tentative pressure of her hand, and she stepped inside. Warmth. She savoured it, stood letting it seep into her chilled body, almost forgetting——

'Who the hell is there?'

She started at the fierce note in the voice. She foolishly knew that she had imagined any vulnerability in the cursing she had heard moments before. She nearly turned and ran. Except that she could not bear the thought of going back out into that cold and relentless night. Fatalistically, she decided she must take her chances here.

She stepped into the kitchen. Stopped and stared at the man sprawled on the floor, twisted with pain. A strong odour of alcohol assaulted her nostrils. He glared at her.

'Argh!' he finally growled, shutting his eyes as if he had just been subjected to the most horrible of apparitions. He seemed to meditate for a moment, and then reopened his eyes and gazed at her with furious question. Her heart hammered painfully in her chest. There could be no doubt left. This man was an outlaw if she had ever seen one. Granted, she had not seen one, not a real live one, anyway. Still, she had seen pictures in history books, been to films. She *knew* what the traditional bad guy looked like, and he looked like this. *Exactly* like this.

She could tell he was tall. She was very good at judging men's heights, and she did it almost automatically, endlessly searching for the man who would not be intimidated by her own great height. This man would not be intimidated by her height, she decided. In these circumstances, that was regrettable. The unfortunate fact was that this man did not look like he would be intimidated by anyone or anything.

Even seeing him lying on the floor, helpless, she could not shake the sensation she was being confronted with real and raw strength. She could see that strength in the line of the long legs, encased by moulded jeans, in the tautness of his plaid flannel shirt where it struggled to contain the broadness of his shoulders, in the ripple of the corded muscles of his sun-bronzed arms.

Her eyes drifted back to his face. There was a hardness there that matched the steel of well-toned muscles. He had very high cheekbones that bore a shadow of dark whisker. His nose was straight, flaring with arrogance and aggravation. His chin was square, and had a distinctly stubborn cast to it. But it was in his eyes that his true hardness lay. There were slanting, as ice-cold and glittering green as emeralds. Outlaw's eyes. That same look in them that she had seen in history books. Hostility. Wariness. His were hooded eyes that hid dark secrets—and, she realised with a stab of startling honesty, dark charms, as well.

There was something in those eyes that was damnably sexy. The challenge. The faint mockery. The mystery. The look of a man who had no patience with convention, who made his own hard rules, who lived by sheer power and guts and recklessness. And, yes, that image had a faint wild appeal, a hint of danger, a sizzle of excitement, that she was positive would have lured many an innocent maiden on to the rocks of his intrigue.

Her eyes shifted uncomfortably from his face, and were drawn to his hair. It was the only thing soft about the man. It was light brown, streaked to honey in places. Somewhat startling compared to the darkness of his beard. Not so startling was the fact that it was completely without style. No, this was not a man who would waste much time pandering to style. His thick mane was long at the back, too long. The front looked as if he'd impatiently taken a pair of scissors to it. And even that could not diminish its lure. His hair softly called to be touched, its texture rich, silky, inviting the exploration of sensitive fingertips.

'Who the hell are you?' His voice was gravelled, from pain or an innate sensuality, she couldn't be sure. But of one thing she was more than sure—it would be absolute folly to tell a man like this who she really was. She could only pray that his lifestyle was as wild and remote as he appeared to be, that he had never seen a picture of Sahara.

'My name's Sarah Moore.' To her dismay, her name came off her own tongue sounding rusty from disuse... distinctly tentative.

Despite the fact that he was in pain, he seemed to possess an animal alertness, because he caught her hesitation, the tentative note in her voice, and held it. His eyes narrowed to green slits of suspicion, rested on her with stripping intensity.

She looked uneasily away from him, remembered suddenly that there might be another bandit in the vicinity. Perhaps even lurking in the shadows of the cabin, watching her.

'Who did this to you?' she asked nervously.

He looked incredulous. 'The wicked witch of the west,' he snapped, his voice a low growl of sarcasm.

Sarah started. For heaven's sake! He was looking accusingly at her! *The wicked witch of the west?* How dared he? She very nearly drew herself to her full height to inform him that he was fortunate enough to be sharing his humble kitchen with a woman who was generally considered one of the most beautiful in the world. Yes! Even since she'd retired from modelling! Wicked witch of the west, indeed!

But caution managed to catch the words before they tumbled off her tongue. No, it would not do for this man to know who she was. He, with dark mysteries glittering in the depths of his jade eyes, would have no conscience about holding her ransom, using her to his greater gain...

'Was it you who laid hammer to that saw blade?'

What did that have to do with anything? 'Yes, but——'

'OK, *Sarah Moore*,' he spoke her name with contempt, as if he had deduced that he had been told a lie, 'I happened to think I was the only human being within a hundred square miles. I happened to be standing on that chair, and on that stack of books, trying to get something out of that cupboard——'

She smelled, again, the liquor so heavy in the air. Glared at him with righteous indignation. 'You were probably drunk. You probably still are drunk. You have the audacity to accuse me of causing you injury, when you drunkenly fell off a chair? You have some nerve.'

His eyes widened with startled surprise, and then narrowed again, even more dangerously than before. 'I am not drunk,' he hissed. 'I was retrieving the bottle, which broke before I had a chance to lay my lips to it.'

'That's a very silly place to keep a bottle,' she said sanctimoniously.

He sighed irritably, and closed his eyes as if to gather strength. *'I have some nerve,'* he muttered. 'Here I am enjoying the privacy of my home, keeping my liquor where I damn well like to keep it, and getting lectured for it by the lady who knocked me off my chair and broke my arm. And *I* have nerve?'

She noticed that he was quite pale, that there was a strained line of pain around his mouth. Perhaps now really wasn't the best time to be arguing about who was guilty of what.

'Do you really think your arm's broken?' she ventured.

'Really,' he confirmed tautly, without reopening his eyes. 'I think my ankle's twisted, too.'

'What can I do?'

The eyes sprang open. 'Haven't you done quite enough?'

'Look, Mr——'

His eyes narrowed on her with cold assessment. She had the discomforting notion that he did not at all like what he saw. A veil dropped over his eyes. 'James,' he supplied smoothly. 'Jacoby James.'

It was a lie. She knew it to the bottom of her toes. Still, the James part was fitting. She christened him Jesse in her mind. Yes, Jesse James was as close to the truth as the name he had just given her. No doubt closer.

'Look, Mr James, I am not going to be held accountable for the fact that you were balancing yourself rather precariously on a rickety chair and a pile of books and fell——'

'—when a sound like a banshee shrieking ripped through the night,' he reminded her, but suddenly he sounded very tired, his words an effort against agony.

'You had better tell me what to do,' she said, feeling suddenly calm.

'Try siphoning the booze off the floor and squeezing it into my mouth,' he suggested, his pain not doing anything to relieve what she suspected was perpetual sarcasm. His face contorted. 'There's a first-aid book on the shelves in the living-room,' he gasped. 'Maybe——'

She hurried into the gloom of the living-room, and squinted at his bookshelf. In a different time she might have allowed herself surprise at the calibre of the reading material he possessed. Now, she only scanned the titles, finally finding a small black book produced by the St John Ambulance Brigade.

She went back into the kitchen. His eyes were shut, his breathing deep and laboured. Had he gone to sleep, or passed out? He'd probably hit his head.

For a moment panic rose in her throat. Certainly nothing in her life had prepared her to deal with any kind of efficiency with medical emergencies. She forced herself to take a few deep breaths for calm and then opened the book.

She dealt with the arm first, amazed at both her steadiness and the competence that the simply written book allowed her to feel. She diagnosed the break as upper arm. She didn't allow herself to consider that she might be wrong. She ripped the sleeve away from the injured arm, and then gently and awkwardly she managed to get the faded flannel shirt off him.

Her eyes caught on his naked chest and she stared helplessly. Lord, but he was a beautifully made man. This from her, who had worked with some of the most magnificently made men in the world. His chest was broad and deep, the muscle of it supremely cut, the colour bronze beneath whorls of silky hair that softened the pure iron of it. Her eyes followed the hair that narrowed to nothing over the flat, hard plain of his stomach. She touched him, her fingers drawn to him, a magnet to steel. She felt relief. A man of flesh and blood after all. The skin was warm and vital, satin beneath her fingertips. The sensation of relief was quickly being replaced by another sensation...

She jerked her offending hand away, gazing speculatively at his face. No witness, thank goodness, to this moment of pure physical insanity.

She turned her thoughts firmly back to the job in hand. She shredded the tablecloth to bind his arm firmly to his chest, and to make a sling. With some grunting and groaning from both parties, she managed to get the first task done.

Next, she scowled at the high cowboy boots that encased his feet and the lower part of his legs. She tugged tentatively at one. It slid off with very little effort and she examined the ankle. Not this one. She tugged at the other boot. He groaned. She tugged harder, feeling the sweat begin to bead on her brow. The boot would not budge, a sure sign that the ankle was already tremendously swollen within it.

She looked around the kitchen with frantic eyes. Her gaze fell on a pair of shears. She had a pair like that in her own well-equipped kitchen that she used to cut up chickens for the gourmet creations she took such delight in preparing. She retrieved the shears and began working on the boot. The shears worked better than she had hoped, but it was still a long and cautious process. Finally she had the boot sliced open and took it off.

She was exhausted and bleary-eyed when she finally finished wrapping the ankle. Jesse was shivering now, and so was she, suddenly aware that her clothes were still clammy and damp from the rain. The fire in the stove had gone out and she had no idea how to restart it, and was too exhausted to rise to a new challenge. She staggered into the bedroom, looking for a blanket for him, and a bed for herself.

The room was very dark. She groped along the wall for a light switch, but found none. She looked back into the kitchen and sighed. There wasn't going to be a light switch. It was a coal-oil fixture of some sort that gave the kitchen light. She wouldn't know how to start such a contraption if she could find it. She squinted into the blackness of the bedroom, made out the outline of a bed, and fumbled her way over to it. She found a single quilt. She debated crawling under it, and leaving him to shiver in the kitchen. She couldn't carry him, after all. She hesitated, and then her conscience won a slender victory.

She took the quilt off the bed and went back into the kitchen, now quaking with both cold and reaction to her night's experiences. Casting him a furtive look, she squirmed out of her damp clothes, grabbed his now tattered shirt, and shoved her wooden limbs into it. She refused to let herself dwell on the fact that the shirt smelled heavenly. Faintly of soap, faintly of sunshine, faintly of that mysterious essence that was man.

She lay down on the floor beside him, pulled the quilt up over them both and tucked it snugly around them. The floor was hard, but she was beyond caring about such petty details. She was warm. For a minute she lay stiffly at his side—but dammit, she could feel the temptation of the heat radiating from that solid body next to her. With a mew of surrender and utter contentment, she pressed into him, and fell asleep with her nose pushed into the hard wall of his chest.

She woke once. The chill grey of early dawn was washing over the cabin. Jesse was restless beside

her. Moaning in his sleep. She caught the words.
A name? Tony Lama. Mumbled two or three times,
with anger.

Mafia, she deduced sleepily. Jesse didn't look
Italian. Not with those eyes, and the soft, honey-
streaked brown of his hair. 'Shhh,' she reassured
him soothingly, still playing nurse to her patient.

He stiffened. Somehow he had forgotten that *she*
was here. A six-hundred-dollar pair of boots lay
beside him in tatters, he was lying on a cold, hard
floor, instead of his own bed, and the pain throbbed
non-stop through his arm and his ankle. His
confused mind had registered each of these things
without recalling her at all. He rolled over to look
at her. His arm screamed its protest, but it wasn't
that that brought the sound to his lips.

'Argh!' he exclaimed roughly.

Her eyes shot open, and she glared at him. He
clenched his eyes shut. This is a nightmare, he told
himself. He opened his eyes a fraction, and peered
at her through his lashes. Her eyes were closed now,
but her lips were pursed in a disapproving and
insulted line. He studied her for a moment. Looked
at the tangle of her filthy black hair and the heavy
black streaks under her eyes and the livid red welts
against the deathly white of her skin. He shuddered, and felt her cringe, and knew she'd recognised the insult...

Well, dammit, he couldn't help it. She looked
like a feminine version of Count Dracula. Maybe,
he thought wearily, she'd been at a Halloween party.
Was it that time of year? He'd lost track of details

like that after he'd been up here for a while. Anyway, it wasn't up to him to protect this intruder from her own sensitivities. Intruder.

He wondered, with a slow fear, how badly he was hurt. It felt really bad, but doctors could work near miracles these days. He'd probably be back at it in a week. He had to be back at it in a week. He was already behind where he wanted to be on this particular 'project'. And it was so easy to lose it, the train of thought, the concentration, the total immersion in his work that gave him that edge.

He stifled a sudden urge to turn around and place his hands around that skinny neck and throttle her. There was no use doing any more damage to his arm . . .

CHAPTER TWO

WHEN Sarah awoke again, the watery grey light was stronger in the cabin. She could hear rain pattering on the roof. She was aware that she was freezing. The body that had kept her so comfortably warm all night had shifted and was no longer touching her. In fact, Jesse was sitting up, his broad and naked back braced against the wall, his shredded boot in his free hand.

Her eyes drifted to his bare torso. She closed her eyes with a shiver of pure appreciation.

'Look what you did to my boot.' He was scowling at her. She felt anew the impact of his eyes. The strength of him. If anything was left of her Florence Nightingale feelings of empathy, they fled her now.

'Don't you think it would be a little more appropriate to thank me for the bang-up first-aid I administered?' she sputtered.

'Oh, sure. And, while I'm at it, I'll thank you for nearly killing me last night.' His gaze was back on his boot, his expression unbelievably like that of Pooh looking at an empty honey jar. His face had softened with regret over a stupid boot! Well, what did she expect from a backwoods recluse? From a renegade? Warmth? Humour? Compassion? Courtesy? Let him waste his tiny bit of human emotion on a boot. What did she care?

'It's cold in here,' she complained.

'No kidding. You let the fire go out.'

'Look, buddy, I happened to spend a good deal of last night looking after your injuries. And that was after I had just had a bad car accident. Besides which, I wouldn't know the first thing about keeping a fire going. Where I come from we turn on a thermostat when we want heat.'

Her indignant speech was greeted with aggravating silence.

'Where exactly do you come from?' he finally asked. His tone was casual to the point of complete disinterest, but his eyes were watchful on her face. They were the eyes of a wary animal, too oft hunted.

Sarah hesitated. The less she told him about herself, the better. Still, her accent had caused a good deal of interest as she'd made her way across Canada—and its origin had been pinpointed more than once. Besides, it was a very big town. Being from the Big Apple didn't necessarily make one rich and famous.

'New York,' she answered crisply.

'New York?' It came out a purr of pure suspicion. 'And what exactly is a woman from New York doing on a lonely back-road in the middle of the wilds of British Columbia?'

'I'm on holiday,' she said carelessly. 'I was going to spend them with my father. He lives around here...somewhere.'

The light in his eyes was icy-cold and piercing. 'Somewhere? Where, exactly?'

'Exactly why am I being subjected to an inquisition?' she asked impatiently.

'Just answer the question,' he suggested with soft menace.

She could feel her heart begin to hammer. Caution lights were flashing in her head. Everything in his tone, in the fine tension of his body, suggested that this was indeed a man hunted—running from something or someone.

'He lives at Jones Lake. Or maybe Jonas Lake. He has very bad handwriting.'

'You came out here—drove, from New York City—to visit your father, and you don't even know exactly where he lives? This is a pretty big country, Sarah Moore.'

She didn't like the way he'd said her name, with underlying scorn as if it were a pseudonym she'd created for his benefit.

'I happen to know it's a big country,' she shot back. She didn't let any of the weariness she'd experienced in finding out just how big a country creep into her tone. 'And I happen to know exactly where my father lives. He gave me a map.'

'May I see it?'

'It's in the car,' she said.

He nodded. 'In the car that you had the accident in.'

'Why are you so intent on disbelieving every word I say, Mr James?' She placed her own mocking emphasis on the name he had given her.

Which only served to narrow those green eyes yet further. 'You're a long way off the beaten track. This road doesn't come anywhere but here.'

'So I guess I got lost,' she said with impudent lack of apology. 'I don't think that's a crime.' She wished, immediately, she could steal back the word crime. Since she couldn't, she watched his features for reaction. She relaxed only slightly when his expression gave no warning of danger. Because there was something in the carefully schooled impassiveness of his face that told Sarah that this was a man accustomed to keeping secrets about himself.

His eyes remained on her for a long time, his gaze so intense and stripping that she was beginning to feel like a fly pinned to a piece of paper. But she refused to back down from that steady, searching gaze. Somewhere in the back of her mind she had filed a piece of information that told her never to show fear or uncertainty around wild things—human or fur-bearing. They preyed on it. But also, deep in her gut, she really and truly didn't feel afraid of Jacoby James. Given his menacing expression, this was probably most unwise on the part of her gut.

She did not, she reminded herself bitterly, have a terribly good track record in terms of trusting her gut feelings about people. She tried to separate her imagination from her logic and decide how much danger she was really in. She was able-bodied, and he was not. That evened the odds in her favour.

He seemed to abruptly lose interest in her. He tried to get up, and failed. 'I'll need some help,' he requested, without a trace of humbleness.

With a great deal of effort they managed to move him to the sofa. The appearance of this piece of furniture was not improved by strong daylight. It was so faded that the pattern on it was indistinguishable. A spring popped uninvitingly out of one of the cushions.

'What now?' she asked.

'Heat,' he suggested. 'And then a cup of coffee. And then we'll go into town. I think I need a doctor.'

He had a vehicle! The thought hadn't even occurred to her. Somehow she had pictured him riding a prancing black horse, a bandanna pulled up over his nose, six-shooters blazing from his hands. He had a car. It seemed to make him a mortal man, after all. Not the reincarnation of some devilishly enticing legendary bad man. She nearly jumped up and down with delight.

'Why don't we forget the heat, and the coffee, and just go?'

'Fine by me. I thought you might want to tidy up a bit.' It was said with a small effort at tactfulness, and Sarah was momentarily confused. Under the circumstances, surely he wasn't too concerned about her brushing her teeth and running a comb through her hair? And then it hit her. She was still wearing his shirt—and only his shirt. And she had come through a hellish obstacle course to get here last night. She hazarded a glance down at herself, and winced at the streaks of mud and unsightly scratches all over her.

She spun haughtily from the open amusement in his eyes, and stomped into the kitchen. A broken piece of mirror was tacked up over the sink.

She looked into it, her initial dismay giving way to a shout of laughter. 'Argh!' she growled. No wonder! No wonder he thought she was the wicked witch of the west. She had never seen such a sight as her own muddied features looking back at her.

Her hair, usually the rich dark brown of a devil's food cake, was plastered to her head in an unbelievable mass of tangles. It had been robbed of its colour, turned grey with smeared grime.

The effect of her eyes, described in her Press portfolio as the 'stunning blue of star sapphires', was somewhat diminished by the black raccoon-like smudges her mascara had left dripping down her face. The proud line of her nose was obscured by a deep, blood-filled welt. Her high cheekbones were overshadowed by smears of mud, mascara and blood. And she had expected him to recognise her as one of the most touted women in the world? No wonder he had looked at her as if she had been incarnated directly out of a horror film.

She realised that it was going to give her a great deal of satisfaction to turn from an ugly duckling to a swan before his very eyes. And it was going to vindicate her wounded pride enormously when he reacted as every man reacted to Sahara—he'd be panting after her like a dog in the heat of an August sun. And she'd give this rude and boorish man her most polished smile, and her jauntiest wave, and be gone. Leaving him to dream daydreams about her for days and months and maybe even years to come!

'I need a bath,' she said, poking her head into the living-room. He was lying on the couch, his good arm thrown up over his forehead. He peered out from under it with a look of astonishment.

'A bath?'

'I'm not going anywhere looking like this,' she stated firmly. 'Just point the way to the bathroom.'

He sighed—what sounded like a sigh of long suffering. He waved his arm vaguely. 'Over there. Between the billiards-room and the library.'

'Oh, never mind,' she said crossly. 'I'll find it myself.'

He sat up swiftly, and winced in pain from the suddenness of his motion. But his voice was as sharp as the report from a pistol. 'You will not go snooping through my house. There is no bathroom.'

She stared at him. He looked very dangerous again. He was hiding something. What? Money-bags from a bank? The floor plans to a jewellery shop? Weapons? Drugs?

'No bathroom?' she finally squeaked.

'Unless that little building to the north of the cabin counts.' He seemed relatively relaxed again, though the wariness had not left his eyes. 'I guarantee you won't find a tub in there. Of course, there's a lake right outside the front door. A very cold lake, but help yourself.'

She marched by him and looked out of the front window. Her breath caught in her throat. There was a small lake, maybe a mile wide and a mile long, out there. It was fringed by wild trees and rock, and in the background rose mighty mountains. Even on so grey a day as this it was intensely beautiful. It rather made up for the plainness of the house that so magnificent a world waited right outside the door to be discovered. It almost made her hands itch to be on a camera, except, she reminded herself firmly, that she was not a photographer any more, either. Never had been, for that matter.

Since she had never had a childhood in the sense of most children's, she did not know how to swim. Besides which, she did not want to be cold again for a long, long time.

'How do you take a bath when the weather turns cold?'

He hesitated. 'I use the galvanised tub in the kitchen.'

'Fine. That's what I'll use.'

'Do you know how long it will take to heat water for a bath?'

She stared at him in disbelief. Of course she had heard of 'roughing it', but this was ridiculous. 'You don't have hot water.' It came out a flat, incredulous statement, rather than a question.

'No, ma'am.' He said it with a certain satisfaction. 'I don't even have running water. There's a pump.'

'That's primitive.' Sluicing off under a pump was definitely not what she had in mind.

'Yes, ma'am.' A grin actually lit his face. And, as self-satisfied and superior as it was, it was stunning the change that it rendered over those hard features. It was like seeing a flash of sunshine touch a rock, momentarily working magic, turning stone to something soft and warm, golden and inviting. A lethal kind of charm came from him, but Sarah steeled herself against it. She knew about illusions. When the sun went away, the rock would remain, as hard and cold as ever.

'I'm having a bath,' she insisted softly. See how smug and superior he looked when Sahara emerged from that tub!

'Fine. You'd better get the fire going. And could you please make me some coffee while you're at it?'

'Make your own damn coffee!'

'I'm not exactly mobile,' he reminded her. 'How about a trade? You make coffee, I'll lend you some reasonably clean, dry clothing.'

The mocking humour that danced in his eyes infuriated her. She'd wear her own clothes. She looked at the soggy pile on the floor and shuddered. On second thoughts——

'Cream. No sugar.' He lay down again, threw his good arm back up over his forehead, oblivious to the fact that she was looking daggers at him.

The bath did take an incredibly long time. She had to haul in water from outside. Mercifully, the rain had stopped. Then she had to suffer the indignity of him snapping orders at her on how to run his stupid stove. She actually had to chop kindling to get the blasted thing going. Her hands had been protected all her life. Blisters began to form across her palms. Reasonably, she knew she should exercise her woman's prerogative and change her mind. But her pride wouldn't let her. She had said she was having a bath, and she was locked on that course now. She didn't care if it took her until midnight to get that huge old tub filled. And it meant more than ever to her to say goodbye to this man as Sahara. She'd see an attitude change then, she was willing to bet!

It was for that, more than anything else, that she continued to work in furious silence while he sipped leisurely at his coffee. His enjoyment of his coffee had not, she noted with irritation, been noticeably changed by her happily informing him that his imported ceramic coffee mug probably leached killing proportions of lead.

Finally the tub was reasonably full of tepid water. Sarah peeked into the living-room. He hadn't moved, but she suspected that, despite his relaxed pose and closed eyes, he wasn't sleeping. He was too worried about leaving his secrets unguarded, she decided balefully. She helped herself to some clean clothes she'd discovered hanging on a line under the relative shelter of the porch.

'I'm taking my bath now,' she finally called. 'Don't you dare look into this kitchen.'

'Oh, lord,' she heard him mutter. 'I haven't seen enough?'

She smiled with cold anticipation and smugly slipped into the water.

Half an hour later, however, she wasn't nearly as pleased with her transformation as she had hoped to be. His huge shirt had rendered her figureless. His trousers were shapeless on her. There was nothing she could do to cover the welt on her nose as her cosmetics kit was buried out there in the car somewhere. Still, she didn't look like an 'argh' any more. That aura that had made her Sahara, the world's most sought-after model at age fifteen, was in her eyes. It was there in the way her heavy, and now gloriously clean and shining hair swirled around her shoulders. It was there in the fresh flawlessness of her skin. Only the camera, primed for those incredible close-ups, was cruel enough to see the tiny wrinkles starting about her eyes, to see that the skin was no longer as translucent as it had been in her extreme youth. And even the camera was still kind to the perfect structure of her face.

She marched out into the living-room, her head high, her eyes sparking with that look of cool refinement that the photographers loved, because they said it never quite masked the passion, only made it look as if it had to be reached for, sought after, unwrapped. Of course, she had never really seen what the others saw. In fact, it quite baffled her. Maybe that was why, now, it was all catching up with her. She had believed too long what others had told her she was.

'I'm ready,' she announced to the inert form on the sofa.

He lifted his head, regarded her thoughtfully. 'That's an improvement,' he said, his tone strangely gentle.

She stared at him. Unless she was mistaken, and she was sure she was not, there was actually sympathy mellowing those unfathomable eyes, making them warmer and gentler. She wanted to kill him! How dared he not recognise his error? How dared he not worship her with his eyes? How dared he not stutter his recognition of her beauty in an awed, slightly strangled tone?

'You think I'm ugly.' Her thoughts were blurted out with utter and shattered disbelief.

'Now, now,' he said placatingly, 'I didn't say that.'

But his very tone confirmed his reaction. As if she were a very homely girl who had struggled to make herself beautiful, and had failed to the point that she'd aroused sympathy. She would have laughed out loud if she hadn't felt so genuinely offended. Ooooh, the satisfaction it would give her to shove one of those old *Cosmo* or *Vogue* covers under his nose. She would, too. Not now, of course. She was still vulnerable. But she'd post him one at the first opportunity—if places like this got post. She'd have one dropped from an aeroplane if she had to!

The man's taste was obviously all in his mouth. An uncouth, mean-minded mountain man who probably liked brassy blondes who chewed gum and smoked cigarettes simultaneously!

'I'm sure it will come as a surprise to you that some people find me very attractive,' she stated coolly, shoving her nose towards the ceiling.

'Of course that doesn't surprise me,' he said, the undisguised pity of his tone making her want to grab him and shake him until he *saw*. Suddenly, she felt deflated. Why should it matter to her what some rough-and-tumble backwoods renegade saw in her? Or didn't see?

But the look in his eyes was causing her to remember something painful and long-buried. It was as if he had flipped back the years, and had seen the plastered-to-the-wall-flower she had always been. Even after. Even after she had won the modelling contest that had propelled her into the fame and fortune that dreams were supposed to be made of. Her mother's dream. Hers had been the dream of any fifteen-year-old. *Please, somebody, ask me to dance. Please.*

Her mother had made her go to those horrid high school dances. Made her go, though she had missed months of school at a time, and hadn't known anybody. 'Sahara, it's good for your image to appear normal and wholesome.' As if she really hadn't been.

And so she had gone, and had suffered the most unbearable loneliness. The boys too intimidated, by both her height and her fame, to ask her to dance. The girls openly hostile. Saying, just loudly enough for her to hear, 'Well! Anybody could look like that if they had a make-up artist spend three hours on their face.' Inside the most glamorous model in the world, a little girl, so unsure. The little girl still there, only better now at wearing her mask. Why was this stranger seeing through her mask?

Her feelings must have been like an open wound on her face, because Jesse looked truly contrite that he had hurt her. 'Look.' That gentleness was in his voice again. 'I didn't mean to hurt your feelings. You're just not the type that appeals to me.'

'And what type appeals to you?' she asked, her voice cold and controlled and contemptuous.

'I don't think we should get into this,' he warned softly.

'By all means, let's get into it,' she snapped. 'It's not as if anything you could possibly say could hurt my feelings any worse.'

He sighed, obviously recognising that she was not budging until she had wrung it out of him. He closed his eyes, and began to talk, flatly at first, an unconscious enjoyment creeping into his voice at the picture he was creating. 'I guess I like women who are small. Really small. Five feet to five four. And I like them kind of round. Not plump, but all delectable soft curves. I like enormous brown eyes, and blonde hair that floats like a cloud around the face of an angel. I like women who remind me of Persian kittens.'

She felt vindicated. He didn't have any taste!

'I like your voice, though,' he said, opening his eyes again. 'I really like it. It's got a tone, a naturalness, an earthiness that is very appealing.'

Sarah did laugh out loud then. Her voice? The voice that had dashed the career jump from modelling to motion pictures in one sound test? There was something drastically wrong with this man. Drastically.

'Don't worry, dear,' her mother had said, unperturbed. 'We'll get you voice training.'

And she'd done the unbelievable. She'd said no. Just like that. She'd changed everything about herself in one way or another over the years. She'd been blonde, and raven-haired, and red-headed, depending on the shoot, depending on the sponsor. She'd worn black contact lenses, and brown ones, and turquoise ones, and green ones. She'd had her breasts flattened with a binder if they'd wanted the athletic look, and pushed up with a special bra if they hadn't. She'd worn hip padding and rear-end padding, and special shoes that had pushed out her behind. She'd had drops put in her eyes to widen the pupils—never mind if she'd walked around in a myopic haze for days at a time.

And she'd said no, from the bottom of her heart, when her mother had said oh, so casually that next they'd work on her voice. She hadn't wanted to be a film star. She had wanted to do something where she was in control for a change. Where she was telling people what impossible expressions to paste on their faces, what impossible positions to twist their bodies into. She'd picked up the camera. She'd become a celebrated photographer. Never realising, never knowing . . .

'Are you all right?'

She looked at Jesse James. Smiled bravely. She was very good at smiling bravely. 'I'm just fine.' And I'll be a lot better, when I've seen the last of you. 'Could we go?'

'My thought exactly,' he muttered. With her help he made it out on to the porch, settled down into a lopsided seat. 'You'll have to go and get the truck and bring it around. It's in the shed over there. It hasn't been started for a while, so you'll have to let it run. The door on the shed sticks, so you should probably start the truck, and then work on the door.'

'Are you sure I won't be choked to death on carbon monoxide?' she asked suspiciously.

He rolled his eyes with exasperation. 'You could practically drive the truck through some of the holes in that shed. I don't think you'll be in grave danger.'

She looked at the shed. He was quite right. It looked more like a picket fence than a building. For all the dubious protection it would offer a vehicle, she wondered why he bothered. Probably so that anybody trying to find him wouldn't know he was here, she thought with sudden insight, and shuddered. Occasionally, like moments ago, when his eyes had mellowed with unwanted sympathy, like when he had grinned that grin that made him incredibly handsome, it was easy to forget that every indication was that this was a very dangerous sort of man.

Despite the holes in the wall, Sarah found it dark in the shed. She searched for and found the truck lights and turned them on. She felt quite pleased with herself. She hadn't told Jesse James that she'd only had a licence to drive for eight weeks.

And he hadn't told her that the truck was a standard. She turned on the engine, and the truck bucked like a wild horse—right though one of the shaky walls. It careered outside, and crashed against a tree.

His breath caught in his throat, and for a crazy second his only concern was whether or not *she* was OK. For a moment in the house, when she was trying so pathetically hard to look good, he had actually liked her, actually forgiven her for trespassing on his life. Because he had found her oddly innocent, oddly refreshing, oddly vulnerable. Moments like that were rare in life, and he knew you had to pay a price for them. But he'd thought the price was his arm, not his truck.

As soon as he saw her unfold herself cautiously from behind the wheel and come swinging up the worn path towards him, his feelings of concern died with savage abruptness. So did his feeling of having had a special moment because of her. The analytical part of his mind kicked in sharply and he did not like what it was telling him. Because it was telling him he'd been a fool to imagine innocence in the tall and angular woman who walked towards him with a controlled assurance and self-confidence in each step. She reminded him of a panther.

Panthers were not vulnerable, he thought, watching her narrowly. Huntress. What did she want from him?

'Did you damage the truck?' he asked, his tone controlled despite the fury he felt.

'I don't think so,' she offered meekly.

He did not believe the meekness. He did not know what to believe about her. But he had been fooled—and made a fool—before. It wouldn't happen again.

'Look, you're going to have to go back, and try again. Remember the clutch. You have to ease off it, just as you're easing on to the gas.'

'No.'

'What do you mean, "no"?' His every instinct was on red alert now. 'No' with such brazen confidence. Not the same woman who had seemed so vulnerable just a few minutes before. Which was real? He didn't even want to find out. He disliked contradictions. He was extremely good at reading people, and extremely uneasy when he failed to do so to his satisfaction. He wanted this mysterious, irritating, frustrating woman off his property.

'I have just had one automobile accident! If you think I am going to take that vehicle, which I don't know how to drive, out on those treacherous roads, you can forget it.'

'Then what do you suggest?'

'I'm thinking,' she said haughtily.

'Well, let's hope I don't expire while you think. I do have to get to a doctor.'

'I don't think you're in any immediate danger.' Her voice was cross, and then it softened. 'I'm hungry.'

He felt an exasperated kind of fury, because now he could see the contradictions in her in almost every line she spoke. A woman putting him in his place, a child saying she was hungry. A woman-child like this could drive a man crazy in no time. Still, he was hungry, too, and he could tell by the set of her jaw that she was not going to drive that truck anywhere right now.

'We don't have any options, Sarah. You are going to have to drive that truck out of here. Not right now. But later.'

'Couldn't I walk?'

He looked pointedly at the flimsy sandals on her feet. 'I don't think so. Nearest neighbour is about twenty-six miles down that road.'

'Oh, well, Jesse,' she said brightly. 'If I'm going to have to drive, I guess I'd rather do it on a full stomach.'

'What did you call me?'

'Jesse,' she admitted, and then continued with nervous swiftness, 'Sometimes people's names don't seem to suit them very well. You're more a Jesse than a Jacoby, somehow.'

'Is that right?' he said. He could hear the chill in his own voice. He did not like this sensation of not knowing how much she really knew, of not knowing who she really was. He recalled again the hesitation with which she had given her name. No, he did not like much about Sarah Moore—including the fact that there was a small part of her that was likeable. The sooner she was off his mountain, the better.

'Tell you what. You call me anything you like, but you drive that truck out of here this afternoon. Deal?'

'Deal,' she agreed hesitantly.

In fact, Sarah could think of nothing she wanted to do less than drive that truck. Well, one thing— she did not want to stay here with this man who was so sharp and so guarded, so cynical and suspicious. She could tell he harboured a suspicion that she had crashed his stupid truck on purpose, and she did not like the raw tension that his suspicion made her suffer.

She should, she decided, go and get back in that truck right now. But she was hungry. And with horrified fascination she realised something else. Some outlaw part of herself was not quite ready to say goodbye to this renegade.

CHAPTER THREE

'IS THIS all you have for food?' Sarah asked Jesse disapprovingly. Her sole hobby was transforming calorie-conscious food into creations not only edible, but delectable.

He was sitting at the kitchen table, his brow furrowed over a book that looked like very heavy and hard reading. A cheap novel or western would have suited her image of him better. She decided, hopefully, that he was trying to impress her.

He glanced up. 'What do you mean, is that all I have? The cupboards are practically bursting. The fridge is overflowing.'

She wrinkled her nose. 'But not with real food.' She opened a cupboard, peered back in disdainfully. 'In here we have thirty-two tins of canned stew, and four boxes of potato chips.'

'I wasn't expecting a guest,' he said sarcastically, 'and *I* happen to like tinned stew.'

'You like this?' She gingerly picked up a can. 'Poison. Pure poison,' she muttered, starting to read the list of ingredients out loud.

'Spare me,' he pleaded. 'Just pick something out of the fridge, if that doesn't suit you.'

'It's worse,' she claimed, with a sad shake of her head. 'Haven't you heard about red meat, for heaven's sake? You should really make an effort to put living foods in your body.'

'Living foods?' The firm line of his mouth quirked upwards mockingly. 'Pray tell me, what is a living food?'

'Well, you know, lettuce and bean sprouts and spinach.'

'Ah. The dreaded green stuff. I don't want to be the one to break it to you, but it seems to me that as soon as your lettuce is viciously ripped from its life source—the earth—it's as dead as my steak. Slaughtered. Perhaps you could start a group. Prevention of cruelty to lettuce.'

He was making fun of her and there was absolutely no sense in talking to the man, she decided blackly. Why should she care if he developed high blood-pressure and a heart condition in his old age? That would be the problem of some kittenish blonde.

Sarah was famished and the stew smelled savoury as it bubbled away on the stove. It tasted even better than it smelled. Jesse grinned fiendishly at her as she soaked up the last drop of juice with a slice of white bread. She swallowed her sigh of contentment. Debated whether she felt guilty or not. All those calories and chemicals. She thought how horrified her mother would be. And reminded herself, firmly, that it was her life, and banished her watching mother from her brain. Having done that, it was relatively easy to open a bag of potato crisps, which she munched with pleasure as Jesse tried to explain the intricacies of a standard transmission to her. He went so far as to insist that they build a mock-up.

'OK, this one is the clutch,' he said, pointing with a stick to a piece of cardboard, balanced like a see-saw, on a tin. 'This one is the brake, this one is the gas.' He handed her the stick. 'This is the gear shift.' He scrawled a diagram of the gears on a piece of paper.

'Gear shift in neutral, please.'

She humoured him, because the potato crisps had put her in a very good mood.

'Clutch in.'

She rolled her eyes and pressed on the clutch.

'OK, shift into first, and gently put your foot down on the gas, up on the clutch...no, no, other way...you're not stamping slugs, for heaven's sake, gently...try it again...for goodness's sake, Sarah, this is *my* truck we're dealing with...'

Finally, he seemed slightly satisfied. He gave her back the keys to the truck with a slow, reluctant shake of his head. She helped him back outside on to the porch.

Aware of his eyes boring into her, she climbed back into the truck and inserted the key into the ignition, reciting a litany of instructions in her head. All for nought. The truck did not start. The engine did not so much as turn over. She tried several times. Even from a distance she could see him glowering, shaking his head, hear him shouting instructions. She wondered if it might not be safer just to get out of the truck, give the cabin a wide berth and find the road she had come down last night. A twenty-six mile trek in sandals seemed like a lesser evil than facing an enraged outlaw.

She slipped out of the truck, looked around for an exit, and knew she was being silly. He wasn't going to hurt her, after all—at least, not as long as she could outrun him—and that should give her several weeks.

He greeted her with stony silence.

'It won't start,' she supplied.

'You left the lights on. Didn't you?'

She started. She *had* turned the lights on in the blackness of the shed. She hung her head.

'Don't waste that look on me, you conniving Amazon! What do you want here?'

She met his blazing gaze with genuine astonishment. 'Nothing. I told you. I got lost. I had an accident.' *Amazon?*

'Sure. And I'm the tooth fairy. You want something, all right, and that's why you deliberately sabotaged our effort to get out of here. Who are you, and what do you want from me?'

'Want from you?' she snapped. She looked, with deliberate scorn, over his shoulder at his crumbling cabin. 'It doesn't look to me as if you have anything worth wanting. Believe me, I don't secretly covet thirty-one cans of stew.'

He did not rise to her biting wit. He did not even seem remotely amused. 'Then what do you want?' he asked again, the coldness of his words spreading a chill along her spine.

'The only thing I want is to be relieved of your boorish company. And the sooner the better!'

'That's easy,' he said smoothly and coldly. 'Start walking.'

Her mouth dropped open. He couldn't mean that. She searched his remote, rocky features for a reprieve. There was none. He meant it. She stared down at her sandals. Her mind darted down that twisting road, and fear somersaulted in her stomach. She would probably still be walking when night fell. Cold. Alone. Afraid. Tracked by bears. Wolves. Cougars. Bandits.

She turned swiftly away from his gauging, unsympathetic eyes. Damn it, she might die, but she intended to do it with pride.

Or try to. Her shoulders shook. A loud sob hiccuped from her as she walked away.

'Oh, hang on,' he growled.

She stopped, torn between pride and hope. She really couldn't walk to the nearest house. She really couldn't beg him to let her stay, either.

'If you'll find me a couple of sturdy branches, I'll make a crutch. Maybe we can fix your car.'

She turned and looked back at him searchingly.

'Don't think it was your tears that moved me.' His voice was harsh. So were his eyes. 'I'm quite accustomed to dealing with women who are consummate actresses. But I'd rather not be stranded here with a broken arm until someone comes in search.'

Cold fury boiled through her veins. But she smiled sweetly at him—doing justice to the label of consummate actress. She went in search of some sturdy branches for him, feeling an all-consuming and cold hatred. So, he was determined to believe she'd engineered her arrival here, was he? Well, let him struggle over to the car, only to find it would take a better 'actress' than her to engineer a complete wreck.

She turned away from him as he began binding the branches together in a rough approximation of a crutch, because she was certain her pure hatred of him must be shining in her eyes. The ego of the man! Who would go to all this trouble to spend time in his dubious company! Unless it was somebody who wanted information from him. A spy. Did he think she was a Mafia moll?

'I'm ready,' he said grimly.

She smiled sweetly, through clenched teeth, and set a killing pace over the rough terrain she had crossed last night. She glanced back now and then. He was having a very tough go of it, stopping often, wiping his brow, his face contorted with pain. Good, she thought, not in the least tempted to tell him he was not going to be able to fix her car once he got to it.

She reached it ahead of him. Inspected it carefully. It looked worse in the light of day than it had last night. She'd been very fortunate to survive. She inspected the boot again, hoping that in daylight she would be able to figure out how to get it open and rescue some of her clothes. At least her underwear! And just a tiny bit of make-up to cover the unsightly scratch on her nose. She had resigned herself to the fact that the boot was not going to be opened ever again, when Jesse broke out of the woods.

She straightened, folded her arms over her chest and glared caustically at him. She felt thoroughly vindicated by the expression of total and stunned astonishment on his face.

'Oh, I do hope you can fix it,' she cooed, her tone as close to kittenish as she could manage without throwing up.

He turned those slanting green eyes on her. She expected that he would be furious that she had forced him to come all this way without ever suggesting that her car was sitting on its roof, crushed almost beyond recognition.

But there was no anger in his eyes. Just puzzlement. A puzzlement that seemed to go clean through to his soul. 'You really did have an accident,' he murmured.

'I have no reason to lie to you.' Nor you to me, she wanted to add, but didn't.

He sank on to the ground, a grey pallor of exhaustion haunting his features. 'There was something in the way you said your name,' he said tiredly. His eyes were on her face again. Full of a vitality that was not reflected in the rest of his sagging frame. 'Is it your real name?'

She nodded. 'Is Jacoby James yours?'

The suspicion leapt in his eyes again. 'What would make you ask that?'

She shrugged. 'Something in the way you said it.'

He look he gave her was long and hard. He made no attempt to answer her. Eventually, his eyes returned to the car. 'I guess you can forget salvaging anything.' He frowned thoughtfully. 'Nice car. It looks brand-new.'

'It was,' she said, and felt a stab of sadness. It was the only major purchase she'd ever made entirely on her own. Without relying on her mother's, or Nelson's, impeccable taste. It had been the first totally independent action of her life. And because of that she'd become very attached to the car in the few weeks she'd owned it. She'd talked to it, treating it like a conspirator in an adventure. Now it was wrecked. She hoped that wasn't an omen. She suspected it was. She'd tried her wings, and look where it had landed her.

'What are we going to do?' she asked desperately, the full impact of leaving those truck lights burning finally hitting her. She was stuck here. They were stuck here. For how long? How were they going to get out of this mess?

He struggled to his feet. 'We'll have to figure out a game plan. I was supposed to meet a business acquaintance in town in a few weeks. When I don't show, I imagine he'll come looking.'

'Oh,' she breathed with relief. For a moment she had actually pictured them dressed in furs trying to survive the infamous Canadian winter. A business acquaintance? She slid him a look. 'What kind of business are you in?' she asked conversationally.

His face closed. 'Let's start laying down the ground rules right now. We're stuck together. That doesn't give you the automatic right to probe into my personal life. Understood?'

'Actually, I don't think there is much about your personal life, or you personally, that is of the least interest to me, Jesse,' she managed with strangled restraint.

'Good, I feel the same about you. We'll share the cabin, clothes, food. Other than that, stay the hell out of my way.'

'With pleasure,' she muttered, and, without waiting for him, strode back towards the cabin.

But she didn't walk quickly enough that she couldn't hear him complaining to the heavens about the unfairness of being stuck with a female companion he hadn't ordered, who was tall and angular and about as sexy as a washboard.

She considered that twenty-six-mile walk. It might leave her bruised and abused physically, but that misery might be preferable to trying to share such close quarters with the abrasive and secretive backwoods villain. She forced herself to be realistic. At least Jesse was a known quantity—sort of. At least she was fairly certain she could survive his brooding, untouchable nature. Unfortunately, she couldn't say that about a hike through an unknown wilderness.

'Hey, and don't start rifling through my stuff in the cabin, either!' he shouted after her.

'Better get a move on, Jesse,' she called back, tauntingly. 'I could have your whole secret life uncovered by the time you limp up that hill.'

To her delight, he tried to move faster, and fell over. She laughed. And she made sure that she laughed loud enough for him to hear her.

'Do you want to play cards or something?' she ventured that night. Jesse had retreated behind his book and stayed there, even during dinner. She was beginning to suspect his interest in it was authentic, and that he was genuinely uninterested in her.

She had succumbed to the steak in the fridge for dinner. It had been excellent. And Jesse had admitted, grudgingly, that she was a good cook.

He glanced up at her. Put down the book. 'Let's get something straight. Your arrival here has already disrupted my schedule for the entire summer. I am not a happy man. I do not want to pretend I'm happy. I didn't invite you here. You inflicted yourself on me in the dead of night, and caused me grievous injury. I don't plan to entertain you. I don't plan to even acknowledge that you're here. Clear?'

'You're a boor,' she said calmly.

'So I've been told,' he said, picking up his book and ignoring her.

She stuck out her tongue at the cover. That felt quite good, so she crossed her eyes. That felt even better, so she crossed her eyes, put her fingers in the corners of her mouth and wagged her tongue at him. That was when he decided to glance up.

'Oh, lord,' he muttered caustically, 'I know I haven't led the best of lives, but I did nothing, absolutely nothing, to deserve this.'

Blushing fiery red, she quickly got up from the table and went outside. She found an old rubber ball and delighted in throwing it up against the wall of the house over and over again.

'What about sleeping arrangements?' she asked later, when she re-entered the house.

He scowled. To her chagrin, he had obviously not spent a single second trying to figure out how to lure her into bed. Men *always* did that.

'I'll take the couch,' he decided. 'You can have the bed.'

She was startled by the selflessness. 'Thank you.'

He set down the book. 'Do you feel like making cocoa?'

She thought of the calories—almost from habit— and then grinned. 'Sounds good. How do you make cocoa?' Was this a peace offering of types? She knew he couldn't be as good as his word and ignore her for several weeks. He couldn't. She was rather accustomed to her life being a breathless whirl, with herself at dead centre. She thought there was a possibility she might go crazy spending weeks in an isolated spot like this with no one to talk to. To listen to her. She didn't even care if he was an outlaw, a notorious criminal, a pillager...

'You've never made cocoa?'

'No,' she said, and the laughter was gone from her voice. 'I've never even tasted cocoa.'

'I can't believe that,' he said incredulously. 'Weren't you ever a kid? Where did you grow up, on the moon?' A contrite and sympathetic light suddenly dawned in his eyes. 'I'm sorry. Now I really am being a boor. Are you diabetic?'

She shook her head, her face frozen. Her feelings locked in, and his probing gaze locked out. No, there had been no cocoa. Or popsicles. Or pizza. She had become the family bread-winner very, very young. You didn't risk that over a pimple, or a dimple of fat in the wrong place.

'The recipe is on the box,' he said gently.

'Fine,' she said curtly, but she was grateful, too. Grateful that he was being tactful, and not probing the hurts of her missed childhood.

He watched her make cocoa. 'How old are you?' he finally asked.

'Twenty-three.' She felt gleeful. He was getting personal despite all his resolve.

'Really? You look younger.'

Not to the camera, she thought.

'You act younger, too.'

'Do I?' She was genuinely startled. She had been complimented for her maturity all her life—as if it had been a compliment for a child to act like an adult.

'Not very many twenty-three-year-old women would throw a ball up against a wall for two hours just to see if they could annoy somebody.'

She started to deny it, then stopped herself. She had been trying to irritate him, originally. But then she had just played ball. The girls in primary school had always played a game called seven-up. She had watched with wistful eyes, but had never been asked to play, never had the confidence to pick up a ball and play by herself. Even then, she'd been a pariah. A child model. Winning local beauty contests, being the star of ad campaigns like Little Miss Grape Juice. She had never been a child. Never. And when she'd found that ball, something in her had simply yearned to see if it was as fun as it had always looked. It had been fun. She smiled. Jesse was really seeing the worst in her.

But then, he was seeing her stripped of her mask of sophistication. At fifteen she'd been made up to look twenty and older, and people had expected her to act as old as she'd looked. She had. But when she'd found that ball, she'd felt driven to go back, as if she could capture something long lost . . .

'Tell me what you do for a living,' he invited casually.

She wasn't fooled. So much for the theory that he could hold out for several weeks without getting personal. His voice was silk, his eyes were probing. His suspicion, whatever it was, was not completely gone. He was going to lay that to rest, and *then* ignore her. Or so he thought.

'Nothing personal, remember?' she reminded him brightly. Besides, she hadn't thought of what she would say. She still thought that telling him the truth would make her very vulnerable. You didn't go around telling complete strangers that you were Sahara, and that you'd reigned supreme over the modelling world for four years before retiring. It didn't take the brightest light to add in million-dollar contracts. She was lucky enough, as it was, that he hadn't recognised her.

'Is what you do so secret?' he asked. His tone was softly teasing, but his eyes were not. They were narrow and wary again.

'Is what *you* do so secret?'

His words were measured. 'What I do has left me open to a certain kind of harassment. I think I'm within my rights to try and protect myself from that. After all, I'm not the one who landed on your doorstep under the most unusual circumstances.'

'You saw the car!' she reminded him.

'Yes, I saw the car,' he said, but there was still something unconvinced. 'The fact you got in an accident doesn't mean you weren't coming here, does it?'

'I wasn't coming here.'

'Fine. Why don't you convince me? Just tell me what you do for a living.'

'At the moment, nothing.'

An eyebrow arched upwards. 'Are you independently wealthy then? You drive a pretty nice car for somebody who does nothing.'

Was she being cased? Was he trying to find out if he could do a little dirty work without ever leaving the dubious comfort of his backwoods hideaway?

'No, I'm not wealthy,' she lied. 'If you must know, I used to be involved in modelling. It didn't work out.'

He snorted. 'Now that I can believe.' He shook his head, amused now, rather than suspicious. 'I suppose every woman over five feet ten thinks she should be a model, does she?' He seemed to find the thought of her thwarted dream quite hilarious.

'Does it occur to you that you're being exceedingly insensitive?'

His face grew solemn immediately, though his eyes still danced with mockery. 'I'm sorry. I don't claim to be an expert in such things. You just don't strike me as being model material.'

'Why on earth not?' she demanded, not even attempting to veil her hostility.

'Well, aside from the fact that you're unusually tall, you just don't seem to have that quality of glamour, of cool hauteur, of remoteness that I would think models have. Not to say you're unattractive—as you pointed out earlier, I'm sure some people would find you attractive. But you're not heart-wrenchingly beautiful, and you're really a skinny little twig.'

Oh, the ignorant public, she thought woefully. The camera added an extra ten pounds, fleshing out her spare frame. As for being remote, and haughty, one was many things while one romanced the camera. Anything, in fact, that the photographer told one to be.

'I'll tell you something in perfect confidence,' he added. 'Most men don't find padded bras very attractive.'

'Pardon?' she sputtered.

He nodded solemnly. 'I admit it. I was sneaking a peek this morning. It's against every law of nature that a woman as thin as you would be that well endowed. Men usually guess at these things.'

'Is that right?' she managed to croak. What a vulgar human being! No wonder he didn't find her attractive. He had fixated on one part of her anatomy, and had decided it was false. Obviously the man had been a hermit in the backwoods too long. He was probably bloody desperate! Imagine him looking her over behind her back!

In that light, she decided that it would be less than sensible to tell him she was one hundred per cent the real thing. 'I think you're perfectly disgusting,' she hissed.

He shrugged. 'I'm just a man. Men look. I guess most of them have the good manners not to admit it. But you just seem to want so desperately to be found attractive. I thought I'd mention it, that's all.' He grinned. 'Just look at it as a Helpful Hint.'

She stared at him. Did he expect to be thanked?

'I think I'll retire now,' she said stiffly. If he had been looking he would have seen every ounce of that cool hauteur in her face that he thought a model should possess. He didn't look. He struggled to his feet, and stuffed his crutch under his arm.

'I want to do a few things in the bedroom first.' He clumped away.

He took nearly an hour in the bedroom, moving around noisily. When he finally allowed her in, the room was monkish. Her eyes drifted to a padlock on the cupboard door.

'I think you have a serious problem,' she told him.

'I don't at the moment. Can't blame me for wanting to keep it that way.'

'Can I ask you who you think I am?' she demanded quietly.

For a long moment he didn't answer. When he did his voice was soft and thoughtful. 'I haven't a clue. That's what bothers me. It bothers me a whole lot. I can usually figure people out in a glance. You...you I don't know. One minute you're all woman, one minute you seem to be a child. One minute you seem to be hopelessly naïve, and the next I see a certain world-weariness in your eyes. You're a failed, unemployed model driving a twenty-five-thousand-dollar car. Nothing about you adds up, and I don't like that.'

Without another word, he turned and limped away. She shut the door behind him. Rummaging absently through an assortment of men's clothing he'd left for her, she chose a huge football jersey to sleep in.

He was quite right, she thought, even if he was right in the wrong way. She didn't add up. And people who had sized her up in a glance—and how many hundreds of those had there been over the years—had always been wrong. They had missed something. The essence. The child within. They had seen Sahara and missed Sarah Moore.

For a long time, she had looked through her proofs almost frantically, looking for the one that would have caught it. But no, what they had always caught was exactly what Jesse had just said top models projected. Glamour. Hauteur. Cool self-command. Confidence.

And then, when she had switched to photography herself, she had gone through *those* proofs with a renewed sense of urgency, hoping she would have captured it herself. That the elusive spirit that she knew was within her would enter her pictures, making them vibrant and special. She had even managed to fool herself that it must be happening. The photos sold, didn't they? She had requests from all the top magazines in the world, didn't she?

'You're a fool,' Nelson had said at that last bitter meeting. Nelson, whom she'd thought out of all of them had seen it, and had loved her for it. She had loved him back. For seeing it. Hoping, too, he would have eventually shown her what 'it' had been. Instead he had ruthlessly torn her hope, her belief, away from her.

She was in bed now, brushing desperately at the tears that coursed down her cheeks. Show her what? Her father would know. Her father was going to know where Sarah Moore was. Who she was. He was going to see past the surface image.

And what if he didn't? she thought tremulously. The tears came harder. Then, finally, she was going to have to admit it. She had been created... by the Press, by the industry, by her mother. Moulded and pounded unmercifully to fit a certain slot. There was no Sahara. Perhaps there was no Sarah Moore either. Was that why she always spoke her name with such hesitation? Because she was speaking the name of one who did not exist?

Firmly, she turned away from such utterly depressing thoughts. There was no need to puzzle about herself when she was sharing quarters with an honest-to-goodness mystery man. Exploring his mystery seemed much, much safer than exploring her own.

The night was black, the shadow of a sprawling Tudor-style home emerging from the darkness. And then something else emerging from the darkness. A form, even darker than the night.

Totally dressed in black, his eyes glinting cat-green, matching the grace of his movements as he lightly tossed a rope, and its hook caught on a window-ledge.

He shinnied up the rope with effortless strength, pulling himself upwards with his powerful arms. Opened the french window and slid into a bedroom, his eyes narrowing against a deeper darkness.

A woman sleeping. On soundless feet he went over to the bed, stared down at her. A sudden tenderness mixed with the grim remoteness of his features.

Why, it's me, Sarah thought with sleepy wonder, recognising that she was the woman in the bed. In the morning, she felt the oddest regret that she had not willed herself to stay awake long enough to see which prize the cat-burglar had claimed.

CHAPTER FOUR

THE muffled little sobs finally died, and with relief Jesse swung his legs back on the couch. He had been just about to go to Sarah, to see if he could offer her any comfort. He was glad he didn't have to, though. He was terrible at stuff like that.

'You're a boor,' she'd flung at him earlier, and it was true. His work placed odd demands on him. It warped his personality somewhat. The months he spent in observation and intense interaction with another individual often left him spent and edgy and needing solitude. But he was not so sure that the jump from intense involvement to intense isolation was a healthy one. Whatever few social skills and sensitivities he possessed grew rusty from disuse. Of course, he knew that. He knew he was an absolute bear at this stage of his work. That was why he was here. He knew it, and he did not inflict himself on others while he went through this.

Ha, he thought scowling. It was usually others who inflicted themselves on him. The last one had been the young woman with the green Mustang. She'd recognised him in an LA restaurant and had proceeded to ruin what he had planned as a holiday drive across America. Yes, he'd seen America. With a green Mustang in his rear-view mirror. Not an isolated incident. Before that there had been...

Stop, he ordered himself. He was blaming *her* for all the things that had happened before, and really, it had nothing to do with her. Of course, there were some similarities. She had barged into his life and wreaked complete havoc with his schedule, his deadline. If he was a bear at this stage in the proceedings, anyway, he was an absolute monster when a wrench was tossed into his tightly scheduled plans, his tightly disciplined days.

And, of course, it was only self-protective to be a bit suspicious. He didn't like the New York part. He didn't like the look of the car. And he didn't like the baffling enigma of her. He could feel the anger beginning to tighten in his belly again. What was she *really* doing here? What did she *really* want?

He heard a tiny hiccuped sob, and the anger melted. You're a boor, he accused himself. An insensitive, hard-nosed boor.

The next morning he looked at her over the breakfast table. He felt somewhat startled by the colour of her eyes, and realised that his hostility must have blinded him to her. Her eyes were beautiful. Not just the colour, which was unusual, but the depth of them, the sparkling mystery. He cleared his throat, and forced the words out. 'I heard you crying last night.'

Sarah avoided looking at Jesse—something she'd been doing since she'd joined him in the kitchen for breakfast. Partly because she was seeing a very romantic cat-burglar every time she looked at him. Partly because of his state of undress. She wished, irrationally, that he'd put a shirt on, even though it would be very awkward for him to do so with one arm strapped solidly to his chest. His broad and naked chest was a constant reminder of what a virile man he was. She didn't need reminders. Besides, it was somewhat humiliating, not to mention a brand-new experience for her, to find someone rather breathtakingly attractive when the compliment was most definitely not returned.

Still avoiding the probing of his eyes, she busied herself with her plate. 'I hope I didn't disturb you.' She put some bacon on the tip of her tongue, and groaned. 'Why does everything that is bad for you have to taste so darned good?'

His good hand shot across the table, then with surprising gentleness she found her chin being lifted, her eyes being forced to meet his.

His were different today. That same bottomless green, only different. Not so hard and cold. Mellowed, as though a trace of sunshine had touched the surface of an ice-cold, glacial pond.

'I'm sorry,' he said softly. 'I'm sorry I made you cry.'

She tried to laugh. It sounded like a desperate whinny. 'Don't be ridiculous. You don't have that much power over me. It was just reaction. I was very tired. I'd been through a lot in the space of twenty-four hours.'

He nodded slowly, let his hand drop from her chin. 'I'm still sorry. I've been behaving very badly. I'm a rigid man. I like to be in control of things. That's why I come here. No interruptions. No surprises. Each day unfolding according to my plan.'

He tapped his injured arm lightly. 'And now nothing unfolding according to plan. I guess I'm scared I'll lose it.'

'Lose what?'

The wariness danced in his eyes, but ever so briefly. He sighed, and it was gone. 'Never mind, Just suffice it to say you give an impression of being very strong and sure of yourself. Strong enough, I thought, to resist my jabs. To let me take out my bad temper on you, and then turn around and give as good as you got. I'll probably take my frustrations out on you again, despite my good intentions, despite the fact that I'll try to remember you're not what you appear to be.'

'I've already told you—my bout with the blues had nothing to do with you.' She searched his face. His 'you're not what you appear to be' did not seem to be laced with a suspicious layer of double meaning.

'OK.' But his eyes were still on her face, unsettling in their intensity. Filled with what she could only suppose was unwanted sympathy.

That, combined with his naked chest, made her feel vulnerable. But she knew how to chase the sympathy out of his eyes. All she had to do was show some interest in his personal life.

'So, you come up here. For the summer? You don't live here all year round?'

She'd hoped her curiosity would irritate him. It didn't seem to, though she noted that his reply was carefully measured.

'You can't live here all year round. It's completely snowbound by November.'

'So you come every summer?'

'No.' He hesitated. 'Just when I need to.'

Aha, she thought with satisfaction. He came when he was on the run. When he needed a place to hide. When the law was getting too close. That reminder of his dark side should balance the enticement of his chest quite nicely. She told herself sternly that, in real life, cat-burglars and criminals were not very romantic at all.

'And the rest of the time?' she pressed on, taking full advantage of the fact that he thought she was fragile.

But he was obviously done with being taken advantage of. The veil dropped down over his eyes. 'It depends,' he said curtly.

She nodded thoughtfully, and changed the subject. She had got everything out of him that she was going to for one day. But that 'it depends' said a lot. Probably a lot more than he knew. It told her that he was a man without a home. Without roots. Men like that were trouble. Pure and simple.

'So, what do you do around here for excitement?'

His smile was slightly pitying. 'I come here specifically to avoid excitement.'

Yes, he probably got quite enough of that pursuing his criminal activities.

'There's a row-boat here, though. And a canoe. Lots of trails. Lots of things to look at. Help yourself. You might even find you like it.'

She wrinkled her nose. 'I suppose,' she said, without much conviction. 'Your bookcase is well stocked, anyway.'

'Unlike my bar,' he said ruefully. Those green eyes were uncomfortably intense on her face again. 'Do you like to read?'

She nodded. Oh, yes, she liked to read. Not high drama, though. Not anything that promised glittering glimpses of the jet set or the rich and famous. She liked to read, ever so wistfully, about normal people and normal lives. 'I noticed you've got Harrison Bond's series. I might read those again.'

'You like Bond's books well enough to read them again?' He sounded surprised.

She nodded. 'He does something, I don't quite know what. But he takes that one year out of the life of somebody so ordinary and makes it so magical. My favourite was *Ira Sutherland*. Have you read that one?'

He nodded. 'I've read them all.'

'Well, Ira was such a jerk. Everything you'd expect a long-shoreman to be. Loud. Brash. Hard-living. And yet underneath I felt as if I saw the real man, stripped of all the things his job and his life had made him appear to be. He was capable of such tenderness with his son. And moments, that really were nothing, took on a different light and a different meaning.' She was starting to feel embarrassed. 'Anyway, that's what I like about his books. He shows life as having meaning in these little innocuous events. Do *you* like his writing?'

Jesse shrugged. 'He's OK. I think maybe you're reading more into it than what's there.'

She shook her head with absolute conviction. 'No. Maybe you read less.'

'Could be.' He seemed to lose interest. He picked up his book again, dismissing her.

She stared out over his shoulder, out of the kitchen window. The sunshine was pouring in this morning. He had opened the window behind him, and the air smelled so good. As clean and pure as she had ever smelled air.

She wondered what to do with the day. She slid him a look. No, she couldn't rely on him to help her with it. She was not accustomed to leisure. She was especially not accustomed to leisure without 'things' to help her fill it. Her stereo, her television, her interest in cooking, good restaurants, throbbing nightclubs, plays, films, museums, just people-watching at Times Square. Now what?

She wandered into the living-room, pulled *Ira* off the shelf and took it outside. She sat on the porch seat, but didn't open the cover of the book. There was an unearthly beauty out here this morning. The sun was shining off the lake, and catching on the wet leaves of the trees around the cabin. The birds seemed to be rioting, and there was a quiet hum of insects in the background.

She set down the book, and strolled around the cabin. It really was a humble structure. It was leaning and much in need of paint, and yet quaint and picturesque, too. She realised that anything more assuming would have been out of place in this magnificent wilderness, taking up space that was not rightfully its to take.

She spotted a generator under her bedroom window as she traipsed around the cabin. She paused and looked at it, briefly puzzled. She recognised it as a generator because they often used them on shoots for supplementing natural lighting. But what would it be doing here? Jesse had already told her that the fridge and lights worked off propane. She somehow doubted that he worried about a vacuum cleaner. It was probably for nothing, she decided. It looked old and rusty. It was likely it didn't even work.

She saw a trail leading away from the cabin and, impulsively, she followed it. A feeling of serenity stretched tentatively within her. The sun filtered green and gold through the thick trees. The smell of the wet forest was heavy and heavenly. Now *there* was a fragrance she'd endorse with her name, she thought, and then giggled. Who would buy a perfume called Sarah Moore? And earthy freshness would not be a scent endorsed by the glamorous package that was Sahara.

She walked on, suddenly came to a clearing, stopped and gasped.

In the centre of the clearing a tree had been knocked down, most likely by the rage of the storm. An apple tree, she guessed, though she wasn't certain. The sight was so painfully beautiful that it brought tears to her eyes. The tree was blossoming. In defiance of its own destruction, it blossomed.

She turned and ran back through the trees, burst into the cabin. 'Jesse, come here.'

He looked at her, astonished. 'What?'

'I want you to see something. Please come.'

He sighed with weary patience, set down his book, picked up his crutch.

'This had better be good,' he kept muttering as she took his arm, trying to hurry him through the woods. And then they came to it.

He stopped and stared, then sat down, his eyes glued to the broken, blossoming tree. She sat beside him. In total silence, in total reverence, they looked. Drank in this odd and terrible beauty.

Finally, his eyes sought hers. 'Thanks,' he said softly.

'I knew you'd want to see it.'

'Why?' he asked, with soft puzzlement. 'I don't understand. I haven't exactly been friendly, or even courteous. Why did you think there might be something in this cretinous soul that would appreciate this?'

The question took her by surprise. Why, indeed? she wondered.

'Maybe,' she responded thoughtfully, 'it wasn't even you. It was me. It was too much for me, by myself, you know? I had to share it.'

'Not in any way to deprecate your gift. I'm very glad you showed this to me. But couldn't you have enjoyed it for yourself? Did you need someone else to make it real for you? To validate the strength of your feelings, to make them all right?'

'Oh, shut up,' she snapped, stung. 'What are you, some kind of armchair psychologist?' But he was hitting too close to home. Every single thing he had said had had a grain of truth in it.

He looked suddenly taken aback. He grinned ruefully. 'Sorry. Old habits die hard.'

It was her turn to be puzzled. 'Were you a psychologist? Are you?' That certainly did not fit her picture!

'No! Lord, no. I guess I'm just intensely interested in human motivations.'

'Humph. You choose to live rather a long way from the human race for someone who is intensely interested in human motivations.'

He laughed. It was a rich and utterly masculine sound rumbling from deep within him. Crinkles of good humour deepened around his eyes. She stared at him with shock. Even though she had seen this transformation before, it took her by surprise all over again. For a moment, he looked nothing at all like the deeply cynical, hard man. But she supposed even bandits must have occasional moments of laughter. And she supposed even a law-breaker might be deeply interested in human motivations. More so than ordinary, if he was a particularly smart malefactor, or one who worked the con, feeding off human vulnerabilities.

He had said too much for her to have a shred of doubt left that his life involved something illicit. He made no bones about the fact that he hid something. That his life revolved around intricately planned schedules, that he was unable to claim the security of calling one place home. Still, it was easy to think for a moment that he was just an ordinary man. No, not ordinary. Very, very special. There was hint of something within him just as attractive as the outside wrapping was. But she would do well never to forget the darker side, that there was a deep, and most probably unpleasant, mystery about this man.

They sat for a long time, the silence appreciative and comfortable between them. Finally, he got up.

He touched her shoulder, and she looked up into those eyes. There was surprising kindness in them.

'Next time, Sarah, let it be just for you. The next time you see something so splendid, hoard it to yourself. See it as a gift from God, and know that you deserve it.'

She felt a ripple of shock run down her spine. Jesse was completely defying her attempts to place him in a category. She did not expect sensitivity from him. Nor depth. Certainly not any kind of spiritual dimension. And yet, it would seem, all three were there. It deepened his intrigue, and added yet another aspect to his mystery.

'There's a place for being selfish,' he continued softly.

'I'm sure you could teach me quite a bit about that particular quality.' Her tone was mildly sarcastic. She recognised it as a reaction to the vague danger in seeing a compelling mind inside that awesome body. Her words were a frantic attempt to re-erect the barrier of animosity that had been between them since her arrival. It might not have been pleasant, but it was safe, and whatever was passing between them now, jolting like energy along an electrical wire, was not safe at all.

But the smile only deepened in his eyes. 'I think I could, at that. If I had a mind to.' He turned away. It was obvious he had no mind to. Thank goodness for small mercies!

She lingered longer, finally returning to the cabin when her stomach had moved from growling to howling. After lunch she asked him if he had any paper and pencils.

'That's one thing that is never in short supply around here.'

He went into the bedroom and behind his locked door to get it. The lock on those doors irked her unbearably, and pushed her imagination to new heights. At various times she had placed behind those doors small sacks of exquisite, very hot jewellery; a collection of highly illegal handguns; floor plans of banks, executive homes, and Fort Knox; counterfeiter's plates...

He brought her back the paper and pencils. She took them, dismissed her wild conjecturing about the contents of his cupboard, and went back to the tree.

She lost herself. Night was falling before she looked up. She didn't know where the day had gone. She stared down at the paper in her hand, the drawing of the tree beginning to take shape. She was astonished. It was that good. She remembered suddenly that she had done this often. As a child, as a very small child. Found a strange peace in papers and pencils and creating worlds. She remembered something else. Her mother looking at her creations without interest or with outright disapproval.

'One ne'er-do-well artist is quite enough in this family, Sarah.'

She remembered the day she had shredded one of her drawings, thrown the pieces of paper out of their apartment window, watched them drift down to the pavement like snow. Knowing that her mother had wanted other things from her. Knowing that she could make herself into whatever her mother could love—even if it meant destroying other parts of herself.

Not destroyed, after all, she thought, gazing down at the paper in her hand with pride and affection. Just hidden away until it was safe to come back out.

Jesse was still at the kitchen table, still reading. The light from the coal-oil lantern was burning bright. She sat down, did not mention eating. Had forgotten eating and forgotten him. She worked feverishly.

Finally, finally it was done. She felt something explode within her, when she looked at it. It was there. In this drawing it was there. Her soul. A piece of herself that she'd been looking for all her life.

Jesse glanced up from his book. 'Can I see the completed work of art?'

'No.' She grinned fiendishly at him. 'It's for me. Just for me.' Maybe, when she finally got there, she would show it to her father, the artist her mother had held in such disdain. He would understand, of that she was certain. But she could not show her soul to this baffling stranger. Did not want to. Or maybe she did, and her very wanting had a frightening quality to it. She had trusted too much, been too loyal to those not deserving of either her loyalty or her trust. She felt oddly that she had grown up a great deal in one day. She wasn't quite sure how or why.

'I didn't realise you wanted the paper to draw,' Jesse said gruffly. 'There's art supplies in the cupboard above the fridge. I thought I'd try it once, and discovered my artistic talent ran to drawing stick men. You're welcome to whatever's up there.'

She got up on a chair and rummaged through the cupboard. It was a treasure chest. She couldn't contain her gasps of delight, her muffled squeals of pleasure. There were sketch pads, and pencils, and charcoal, and pastels. She looked down from the chair and smiled ecstatically at Jesse.

He was watching her with the strangest look in his eyes. She couldn't quite pinpoint it. Startled surprise? Yes. Probably the very same look she'd given him when he'd made that unexpected and unsettling remark about her deserving God's gifts.

She felt an oddly dizzy sensation, like a premonition. She had a sudden sensation of *knowing*. That, despite their caution, despite all their intentions, they would come to know each other. Already were in the process. They were seeing fragments of each other's souls. It was very, very frightening.

There was no place to run. Fate had them in its clutches.

She wondered if Jesse felt it, too. How could he not feel a truth so powerful that it had crowded into the room with them like a physical presence? He felt it. Because he got up suddenly, his face a mask, stuffed his crutch under his arm and limped outside. For a long time after she was in bed, she could hear the lonely squeak of the porch seat going to and fro.

'Heaven's, it's hot,' Jesse complained. She could tell he was hot. The sweat sat glistening like oil on the superb cut of his muscle.

'I know it's hot,' she said, 'but please try and be still, or I'll cut your throat.'

'How can you cut my throat? You haven't even put the razor to my face yet. Would you hurry? If you walk around me one more time, looking pensive, I'll expire of either heat or boredom.'

'We could go out on the porch.'

'We could just get on with it.'

She looked hesitantly from his lathered face to the razor in her hand. 'Shouldn't I practise on a balloon first?'

'I don't have a balloon! That's for straight razors, anyway.'

After four days, his beard had been getting heavy and driving him to distraction. His attempts to shave, one-handed, had brought one small nick and a dozen roars of frustration. Finally, she had offered to do it. Now she was sorry. It was altogether too intimate. But not as intimate, she reminded herself staunchly, as washing that broad and muscled back had been.

'You're blushing,' he commented wickedly.

'I am not!' she denied furiously. I'm *flushing*. It *is* hot.'

'Right,' he said drily.

'Pompous, conceited ass,' she muttered, and took the razor to his face.

'Not bad,' he said afterwards, looking at his face in the mirror.

'Considering what I had to work with,' she rejoined haughtily. A bead of sweat rolled between her breasts. She blew down the neck of the voluminous T-shirt she was wearing. 'I'd kill for a bathing-suit,' she mumbled.

'Why don't you go swimming?' he suggested. 'It won't hurt the shirt.'

'I don't know how to swim.'

'Don't you?' He frowned. 'You've never had cocoa. You don't know how to swim. Were you sick as a kid, or what?'

She shook her head mutely. There was too much pain here. And it would take a trust she did not feel for Jesse to tell him about it.

'You know, I tried a couple of times to picture you as a child. I couldn't. I can't imagine you as a kid. Letting go. Laughing.'

'Why would you want to imagine that?'

'It's something I do sometimes. A mental exercise. I try to picture people as children.' He stopped abruptly, she could see a self-censure in his eyes. He thought he'd revealed too much of himself. And yet it warmed her to know this. That this man, who made it his job to be closed and unrevealing, liked to picture people as laughing children. However unintentionally, he had just given her another fragment of his soul to add to her growing—and distressing—collection.

'Do you want to learn to swim? I'll teach you.'

'Careful, Jesse,' she said wryly. 'That could be misconstrued as a nice thing to do.'

'Nah. I'm out of books. Actually, I just brought the one. I didn't want to be distracted.' A scowl crossed his face, a scowl she was growing accustomed to, whenever he reminded himself of how his summer was supposed to be going and was not.

'One book and one bottle of booze. You're a disciplined man, Jesse,' she teased him easily. Recognised the ease, and wanted to raise her caution again. Could not. It felt good to be at home with someone. It was not a feeling she had had often in her life. 'I'd like to learn how to swim,' she decided.

'OK, but I don't want any sass from you. You have to listen, and obey.'

She rolled her eyes, but knew she was being teased in turn. They seemed to be on parallel paths. Were the paths getting closer and closer together?

They walked to the water's edge. He flopped down on the rocky shore, and fanned his injured foot through the cold water.

She stuck her toe in. 'Forget it.'

He reached out lazily, used his crutch as a hook, and dumped her into the water. She rose, spluttering and freezing.

'You're wet now, you might as well learn.'

Actually, she wasn't sure that she learned a great deal about swimming. Jesse's one-armed demonstrations were not overly helpful, and neither were his instructions. But she had fun. Real fun. She was discovering some of the lost magic of a childhood she had never had. She flopped around in the water, glorying in it. She splashed him. She ran, laughing in delight as she pounded through the water.

Finally, breathless, she got out and sat beside him. She yanked the shirt up around her thighs to better feel the warming sun. She loved the sensation of sunshine on her skin. It had always been one of the taboos. Sunshine aged and damaged, never mind how it felt. She had always been forced to view sunny days from the shadow of a broad-brimmed hat. Well, she was making up for lost time now. The last time she'd looked in the mirror she'd been delighted to see that she was sunburnt. And that freckles had darkened across her nose. Her mother would have a fit. Good.

'That was fun,' she sighed, closing her eyes, lifting her cheeks to accept the kiss of the sun.

He didn't answer. She opened her eyes and looked at him.

He was staring at her, as if he had never seen her before. As if he had come into a crowded room and been stopped dead in his tracks by an extraordinarily beautiful woman. She had seen the look before. From so many other men, so many other times. But never when she had looked like this. Tented in an oversize T-shirt, her hair a wet tangle, her skin freckled, her nose sunburnt. And yet the look in his eyes was full of surprise, and a muted desire, as if he had just seen her.

He reached out a hand and touched her cheek, and sparks shot through his eyes. Sparks of desire melting the ice of his eyes, melting the chill off her skin. He dropped his head, grazed his lips across the satiny wetness of hers.

The tentativeness of the gesture was fleeting, gone in a split second, in a lightning flash of white-hot heat. Never had she been more sure of his outlaw heart. The kiss had a savage quality to it, an edge of danger, a sizzle of excitement. For a moment, she was too surprised and too stunned to do anything but take, but then some outlaw part of her answered him.

Reached for his wild heart and grasped it to her, and her lips opened beneath the command of his, as her tongue leapt into the hollow of his mouth and explored his tongue and the hard line of his teeth. Outlaws. Running wild from the world on dancing horses, running into the sun, laughing into the teeth of the dark storm gathering within them.

His lips taunted and teased, commanded and played. And she rode with him. Rode this dancing wild thing within her, throwing open her arms to it, throwing caution and concern to the wind. Feeling a part of her as much denied as the child had been. The woman. The woman of strong passions that the photographers and the world had always seen. The woman who had been alien to her. As alien as the child, leaving her in a half-world of unknowing.

But now she wanted to know. Was driven to know. Was ready to know. She felt his hand slip along her neck, caress her shoulder, the long line of her neck. She felt it dip, dry and hot, against the chill of her skin, leaving a path of fire over her dampness.

She leaned into him, pressing against him with a primal urgency she had never felt. His hand found her breast, and she sighed in an agony of delight.

'Oh, lord,' he murmured. 'You're real.'

The soaring sensation within her ended as abruptly as if she were an eagle in full flight and an arrow had pierced her breast, felling her, throwing her back to the earth with brutal and wrathful force. She shoved herself away from him, her moment in the sun exploded into a thousand tiny fragments of humiliation and anger.

She stared down at herself. The T-shirt, that she had assumed was so bulky and unrevealing, was moulded to her like a second skin. And, of course, had been since the moment she had got wet. So that was what had caused that look of discovery in his eyes, that look of wonder!

Beast. A primal beast. As they were all primal beasts. It had taken him longer to spot it. And he had reacted out of a sheer physical need, a purely selfish need, a purely male need.

She stared at him with cold disdain. He did not find her a beautiful woman. Never had. But he liked a part of her anatomy. It was too repulsive for words, how she felt about him in this moment. How she felt about herself. About how easy she had been. How trusting.

He actually looked hurt and puzzled, as if he thought he had hidden his real motives from her. Did he think she was stupid, on top of everything else?

Wordlessly, she leapt to her feet and ran to the dubious protection of the cabin, tears of humiliation and sadness running down her cheeks.

He did not follow. And she could not know that he sat there, looking at the water as if she still ran in it like a breathless child, a magical thing, a nymph.

CHAPTER FIVE

THERE was a soft knock on the closed bedroom door. 'Sarah.'

'Go away!' She heard the door click open, buried her head under the pillow.

'I think we should talk.'

'Get out of my room, you pillager. You despoiler of women. You scourge of the human race. You——'

'Would you come out from under that pillow?'

'No.'

'Sarah——'

'Scum. Filth.'

'Stop it. We're a man and a woman. It happened. There was nothing scummy or filthy about it. And while we're at it, I wasn't giving anything that I wasn't getting back. At least that was my perception of the situation, warped as it may be.'

'You want my perception?' She pulled the pillow away from her face and sat up, stabbing an accusing finger at him. 'You discovered I had a chest—the real thing. And you didn't have a book to read. You disgusting, vile——'

He cut her off calmly. 'That's not how it was.'

'Oh, really? You have made it perfectly clear, from the moment you first laid eyes on me, exactly how attractive you find me. I'm the wicked witch of the west. I'm the Amazon. I'm the washboard.'

'I changed my mind,' he said evenly.

'My point exactly! You changed your mind in about the same moment that you noticed my curves were the authentic item. You can't imagine how flattering that was for me.'

'Sarah, the first time I laid eyes on you, you looked like something that had been exhumed from a grave. First impressions are powerful. They kind of overlay what is real for a while. But reality has started to pierce that first impression. You actually look very attractive to me, sometimes.'

'You sex-starved deviant!' *Sometimes?* 'What were you going to do when we got down to brass tacks? Ask me to put a paper bag over my head?'

'I wasn't plotting that far ahead,' he said, anger rising in his tone. 'Were you?'

'I most certainly was not.'

He looked at her for a long time, finally limped over and sat on the bed, regarded her with steady and stripping eyes. 'This hasn't got a thing to do with me, has it?'

She moved stiffly over into the corner, eyeing him warily.

'This has a whole lot to do with other people. Other men. Who treated you as if you were a package instead of a person. Am I right?'

She shook her head vehemently. 'No!'

'Let me tell you something, Sarah Moore. For a crazy moment, when you were cavorting in the water like a child let loose, like something wild and free, like a goddess dancing with the sun, I thought you were the most beautiful thing I had ever seen. And it didn't have a damn thing to do with the curves you seem to be so bloody protective of. It had something to do with the light shining in your face and your eyes.

'I made one hell of a mistake, and I don't make them often. But what I thought I saw was pure illusion. Because that woman who danced with the water and the sun is not the whining, self-pitying child who is lying on *my* bed, inflicting her views of me on me after barging uninvited into my life.'

He got up, his face like thunder, and limped proudly to the door. He turned there and gave her a withering look. 'I told you once, and I'll tell you again. You stay the hell out of my way. And consider yourself lucky that I don't kick you out to walk to the nearest place of refuge.'

The door slammed behind him, and she rolled over and punched her pillow. And then smiled. A goddess dancing with the sun? Then she chastised herself bitterly. She had heard every line known to man. OK, that one was more eloquent that most, but she had not a reason to believe him.

And he was right. Men did relate to her as if she were a package. A glossy package with 'Sahara' written across it in glittering script. She had always been aware that the men who had asked her out, who had wined her and dined her, and had romanced her with flowers and chocolates and trinkets, had wanted something other than her company. Wanted the conquest. The ultimate conquest of having had, in every sense of the word, a woman who was so publicly proclaimed as being the ideal woman—ravishing, exotic, beautiful, sexy. She had figured out that men tended to see a high-profile woman such as herself as the ultimate feather in the cap of masculine validation. The proverbial notch in the belt.

Except she never had been. She had never sold that part of herself. She had loved Nelson, and had thought he loved her in return. But part of the reason she had been so convinced that he loved her was because he had never pressed for what the others pressed for. She had foolishly assumed that it was a mark of his genuine liking and respect for her, not of his total indifference.

As for Jesse, she'd stay out of his way all right! And he'd better stay out of hers. Because if he so much as laid a hand on her, she'd scream rape into next week. He could add that to his list of evil deeds—a list that grew longer and more colourful daily within the confines of her imagination.

And yet even as she thought her vengeful thoughts she acknowledged a tiny bud of sadness within her. What had happened today would end the ease that had been growing so naturally between them. She should have felt good about that. All her life her mother had warned her about trusting too easily, about the dangers of her being kidnapped. She had grown up watching people warily, and it did not feel 'right' to be trusting Jesse, especially since she was forewarned that he was not the kind of man you should call 'friend'. He did not trust.

His past was wrapped in dark shadows, his future was hidden behind veiled green eyes. There was not a single photograph in this cabin that suggested he was capable of an emotional tie with another human being. This run-down shanty appeared to be the only place he called home. He had muttered about a man called Tony Lama in his sleep. He used a name she did not believe was his own. He kept a cupboard full of secrets. Yes, logically she was well aware that she should feel only wariness for Jesse. And yet her logic was confused. Because there was another side to this man. He had a certain turn of phrase that was eloquent. There were traces of surprising gentleness in him. He had a razor-edged and challenging intellect.

His very complications made him dangerously fascinating. The very fact that she could not come up with one label that wrapped him up neatly, that answered all her questions, made him a challenge, a mystery that she wanted to solve. And there was something more there, too. An evasive something that made her crave those rare moments of his tenderness.

She knew better. Ladies who loved outlaws ended up with broken hearts and broken dreams. She knew that. She had seen *Butch Cassidy and the Sundance Kid* three times. There were no fairy-tale endings when you loved those who chose to live on the edge.

Love? She wondered where that word had come from. Jesse James was one abrasive, prickly man.

He was secretive, wary, stubborn and insensitive.
She would not fall in love with him.

She fell in love with softer men. Was in love,
right now. Recovering from being in love. With
Nelson. Oh, lord, Nelson, with all his culture and
polish and refinement. Nelson with his maturity and
his gentleness and his silver hair. Nelson who had
never looked at her as all those other men had
looked at her. Had never looked at her just as Jesse
had guessed men looked at her—as if she were a
package, and they couldn't wait to get the wrap-
pings off.

Nelson, whose gentle kisses had made her feel
loved, but not threatened by fire. And Nelson the
betrayer, who had laughed at the proclamation of
undying love and forever she had finally had the
courage to give after seven years of rehearsing.

Nelson, who had condemned himself out of his
own mouth, with no apology. 'My dear, I am an
old man. A fading star, a has-been, who basked in
your limelight for far longer than was ethical. I used
you as we all use you. As you beg to be used by
yearning for love and approval. If I have any real
affection for you, and I am really not sure I am
capable of such an emotion, see it in this gesture.
I will not marry you.'

It would have been quite cruel enough if he had
left it there. But he felt compelled to unearth that
other illusion for her. And she had felt compelled
to show him how wrong he was.

He had not been wrong, and, with the world
crumbling, in a fit of despair and pique she had

taken driving lessons, bought a car and headed for Canada. Not telling anyone where she was going or why, only that she was going.

She had a strange surging sensation that told her she had already arrived at exactly the place she was meant to be. But that was ridiculous. Her father was not here. All that was here was an obnoxious cabin mate, and her. Sarah Moore. She was foggily aware that the name felt as if it belonged to her.

Jesse was fiddling with a radio and smoking a pipe the next morning when she entered the kitchen. She had planned to totally ignore him, but didn't quite pull it off.

'I didn't know you smoked,' she said disapprovingly. 'It's very bad for you.'

'Consider it a preventative measure that may be very good for you.'

'In what way will breathing in your stinky fumes be of any earthly good to me?'

He clamped down hard on the pipe. 'It might prevent murder.'

She blanched. Murder? The word had slipped off his lips with relative ease. 'I don't believe you're capable of murder,' she finally said staunchly.

'Oh, thank you so much,' he said with blistering sarcasm. He glared at the squawking radio, and reached for a lighter to relight his pipe.

She cringed. 'Did you know those lighters are very unreliable? That they can blow up with no warning?'

'Where do you get all this stuff?' he demanded.

'What stuff?'

'So far you have seen the potential for perishing in poisons in the food, the dishes, carbon monoxide from the truck——'

'Well, while we're on the subject, has the stove pipe been cleaned recently? I read somewhere once about creosote building up——'

'It's been cleaned,' he snapped with exasperation, taking a strong pull of his pipe. He turned his full attention to the radio. A station was coming in. He got himself a bowl of cereal, too proud to ask her to cook, and went and sat, engrossed in the radio, at the table.

She decided to cook herself bacon and eggs. She hoped he drooled.

'No wonder I come up here,' he muttered to himself after a few minutes. 'You want a recipe for mental health?'

'Not particularly,' she said, sitting down and feeling quite smug at the way his hungry eyes were fixed on her plate.

'Never listen to the news. Or read the newspaper.'

It was the exact opposite of what she'd been told all her life. She wondered if he would write that down and sign it in blood so that she could present it to her mother. Mother's rule was, 'Always read the newspaper and listen to the news. You need to appear informed. You must always have current events available so you can talk to people.' Unsaid: you moron, if we leave you to your own conversational devices you'll bore people. Say the wrong thing.

'Why do you say that?' She picked up a piece of bacon and nibbled on it daintily.

'Huh? Oh, hell, it's so stupid. I mean, is any of this stuff about things you need to know? Is there any reason a housewife in Canada has to know about a murdered policeman in New York, an overturned school bus in Mississippi? You know what depresses people? Makes them afraid to grab life with both hands and live it? Thinking they can't change things. Thinking they're powerless. And that's one thing about the news. You can't change a single thing in it. It's already happened, or it wouldn't be news. It's over. And there's nothing you or I can do about any of it, anyway.'

She glared at him. Why did she think this little speech was connected to all her fears about exploding lighters and leaching plates?

She handed him a piece of bacon when she couldn't stand the look in his eyes any more.

'There's something to be said about being informed, isn't there?'

He shrugged. 'A very wise man once said to me that we're all confused. That we confuse information with knowledge, and knowledge with wisdom. I concur.'

'I happen to think it's important to know about exploding lighters.'

'Do you? Why? You don't even smoke.'

'Well, no, but I want to be able to duck if the one next to me goes off.'

'You can spend a lot of life ducking from fire-crackers and backfiring cars, Sarah.'

'I don't think we're speaking to one another,' she remembered peevishly.

'Oh. That's why my ear is nearly worn raw.'

'I haven't been doing the talking. You have been inflicting your ridiculous philosophies on me, and what's more——'

'Shhh. Do you know her?'

'Who?'

'The missing model. Samantha or Samara or something like that.'

Her whole spine stiffened. She was sure the blood drained from her face. How could he listen to the radio and carry on a conversation at the same time? She handed him another piece of bacon. 'I might know who they're talking about, vaguely. What did it say about her?'

He shrugged. 'Nothing. She's missing. The police don't have any clues, but don't suspect foul play. Feather-head probably forgot to tell her agent she'd booked two weeks at the spa.'

Feather-head? 'Probably,' Sarah responded tightly. She was going to kill her mother when she saw her next. She had told her she was going, that there was no need to worry, that she didn't know when she'd be back. Not that her mother would be worried about anything except her own hide. Not that her mother was doing anything but milking the moment, keeping 'Sahara' in the public eye until the real item turned up again. Which was going to be never. She hoped.

She sighed. Her mother had a way of draining her strength and her resolve, making her see things her way. Her father, she reminded herself, was going to make her strong. Strong enough to stand up to her mother—just the way he had all those years ago. She wondered if that meant she'd be living in the Canadian wilderness for the rest of her life, too?

'Could I have the rest of that bacon? If you're not going to eat it?'

She shoved the plate at him.

'Want to talk about what happened yesterday?' he asked casually.

'No!' She picked up his pipe, pointedly took a mighty pull on it, and then gathered up her sketch pads and supplies and marched out into the bright sunshine. She could hear him chuckling behind her.

She spent the entire morning sketching. It seemed to her that she was able to do with these pencils and this paper what she had tried to do with the camera, and failed to do. Miserably. Or so she had found out. Actually, at the time she had thought she was doing quite well.

She picked out small and innocuous things to put on paper. Things she probably would have walked by without noticing a few days ago. A flower growing out of rock. A single branch of a pine tree. It seemed to her, when she looked at the drawings, that she was managing to do exactly what Harrison Bond had done with his *Year in the Life* series. She was capturing the magic in the ordinary. She was beginning to wonder if that wasn't the only place where *real* magic existed.

She went back in for lunch. Jesse was struggling awkwardly with trying to put butter on bread. She didn't offer to help. He didn't ask. She made herself a thick pastrami and mustard sandwich and was munching happily before he even had his bread buttered. She noticed several massacred slices on the floor. She giggled.

'I'm glad you find this amusing.' He finally thumped over and sat across from her at the table. He picked up a book, shutting her out.

'I thought you didn't have any books.'

'I've read everything on that shelf at least three times. I guess I'll go for four.' He shook his head. 'What a waste. I have important things to be doing.'

'You know, if you'd lower your guard a bit and tell me what you'd like to be doing, maybe I could help you.' Oh, lord, what was she doing? Next thing she knew she'd be an accomplice in the robbing of Fort Knox. Still, she was burning with curiosity. She wanted to know his secrets.

'Nice try.'

'I was being nice,' she said defensively.

'Oh, sure. You won't lift a finger to help me make a peanut-butter sandwich, but you're pretty eager to help me with my work. And I'm supposed to believe you're being altruistic?'

'What do you think my motive was? You, who are so into human motivations?'

'I haven't quite figured that. Your interest could be innocent. The typical woman, putting her nose in everywhere it doesn't belong. But even if it is, Sarah, I don't know who you are. And I'm not giving you any information that you could use to club me with later.'

'Is your life so sinister?' she asked quietly.

He did the unexpected. He threw back his head and laughed. 'Sinister? Honestly, Sarah, you are the funniest, most baffling woman I have ever met. I'll never figure out what goes on in that head of yours. Sinister!' He snorted with laughter.

She watched him narrowly. A smoke-screen. Or was she that far off on the wrong track? No. Just yesterday she had made that long list of reasons of why not to let down her guard around this man. She would not allow herself to be charmed or cajoled into changing her mind. When he presented her with concrete information that explained his locked doors and locked eyes and locked life, then maybe she would believe the easy laughter of his response to the word sinister.

She finished her sandwich. 'I'm going back out.'

'Do you want to row across the lake? To the little island?'

'With you?'

He sighed. 'No. With Marvin the Cow. Of course with me.'

'There's no need to treat me as if I'm stupid.'

'Let me try this again. Sarah, I can't get very far on my own. I am beginning to feel like a caged tiger. Would you please row me across the lake to the island? A small outing for the invalid? Please?'

'I don't know whether I can trust you.'

His face became hard. 'Sarah Moore, I wouldn't touch you with a ten-foot pole.'

At least in that, she thought, with the oddest little twinge of regret, there could be absolutely no denying his sincerity.

'Sure, then. I've never been in a row-boat.'

A few minutes later, they were seated in the boat. It was harder to row than she would have ever expected. She kept splashing him with the oars. Accidentally. It annoyed him so much that she started doing it on purpose. They had a few false starts—she rowing the boat in circles, while he yelled at her how to do it. She rowed the boat in circles a few more times, just to let him know she wasn't intimidated.

Finally, with the sweat running down her and her breath coming in ragged gasps, they approached the picturesque little island. Her eyes roved to Jesse. He looked as contented as she had ever seen him. His broad chest was exposed to her, drops of sweat tangled in the thick hair of it like diamonds. His hair glinted brightly in the sunshine. His eyes were closed, and his face was in complete repose. With the harsh lines of cynicism erased from his face he looked exceedingly attractive. She made herself force her eyes away.

'Jesse!' she shouted. 'Look!'

'Sit down! Sarah, sit down right——'

She was gesticulating wildly at the deer she had seen on the shore. She could hear him ordering her to sit down, but he was always giving instructions about something. The boat swayed. Too late, she realised that she had unbalanced it. She could hear Jesse's yell and then they both hit the water.

She couldn't swim. Panic rose in her throat, and she thrashed around in the water, then realised that the life-jacket he had insisted she wear was holding her up nicely. And at the same moment realised that he hadn't been able to get one over his sling. Remembered his arm bound tight to his body.

'Jesse!' she screamed.

'I'm here,' he said quietly.

The voice came from the other side of the boat. She managed to bobble over. Jesse was clinging to the side, with one arm. Her sensation of relief was so intense it made her feel faint.

'Sarah, we're only a little way from shore. Find the rope at the front of the boat, roll over on your back and see if you can pull us in.'

She nodded, his absolute calm reassuring her. She did as she was told, finally found firm ground under her feet, and breathlessly hauled the boat into shore.

Jesse crawled over to her. She began to cry. He managed to get himself sitting up, pulled her with all the strength of his good arm into the wall of his chest, stroking her hair while she cried.

'I nearly killed you,' she sobbed. 'I could have killed you.'

'Shh, Sarah. You didn't, though. You saved me. We're both a little wet, that's all. It's OK.'

'We both could have died,' she said dazedly, looking out at the innocent water, the beauty of the day, shivering uncontrollably.

'We didn't die, Sarah. We didn't even come close. Let it go.'

'Don't you understand?' she whispered. 'It's scary how fragile it is. How you can be here one minute, and the next minute your car turns over and squashes you, or you fall out of a boat, or a lighter explodes...'

'Sarah, no one ever knows what the next moment holds. That's why you owe it to yourself to live only this moment, live it with all your might. I'm a fatalist. When you're number's up, it's up. If life has reason, so does death.'

'And if your life doesn't have reason?' she whispered.

'Oh, Sarah,' he said, his voice gruff with exquisite gentleness, 'don't you think your life has reason?'

'Well, if it does, I can't think what it might be.' She said it carelessly, but her tone obviously did not fool him.

'Searching for meaning is reason. You are searching for something, aren't you?'

She nodded pensively. 'I think my father knows something I need to know.'

'Ah,' he said, his tone mildly mocking, but still affectionate. 'In the backwoods of Canada searching for meaning. You are beginning to make some sense to me.'

'Am I?' she said hopefully.

His hand traced the curve of her upturned cheek. 'Don't ask me who you are, Sarah. Don't ever ask anybody else who you are, or what your reason is. Answers to questions like that aren't out there, somewhere.' He pressed his hand gently to her heart. 'They're in here.'

She stared into his eyes, hypnotised by the gentleness there, by the caring. She felt herself leaning towards him, as if pulled by a magnet. Her eyelids pressed downwards until she was looking up at him through a fringe of dark lashes. Her lips parted, and her tongue moistened them. She became suddenly aware that his hand still rested with electrical intimacy in the hollow between her breasts. She jerked away from him, and glared at him accusingly. He removed his hand as if he wasn't really even aware where it had rested, but his eyes remained on hers.

'I think I'm going to kiss you,' he murmured huskily.

Her eyes fastened on his lips, and for a moment she felt again the intensity of that feeling that she had thought was relief. But they were both safe, now. Or were they? The feeling was too strong. It swept through her, and she felt as if she would be obliterated if she did not break its spell. And she no longer entirely trusted the idea that the light that danced through his eyes like sunshine was simple caring.

She leapt to her feet. 'Ha! You'll have to catch me first.' She dashed into the woods. She frantically explored the tiny island, and eventually her jangled nerves were soothed by the silence of this place, the utter tranquillity of it. Every now and then she would find a break in the trees and look down at Jesse stretched out on the beach. He didn't seem the least perturbed that she had taken off. He looked like a big contented cat lazing in the sun.

What had he meant, he was going to kiss her? Had he been teasing? The look in his eyes hadn't been teasing. She shook her head. Jesse found her attractive at the oddest times. Honestly, he was one weird man. One weird, attractive man. She had been able to run from his lips this time. But it had taken every bit of her strength. Heavens, she was dreaming about the taste of those lips at night. If she went back, and he still wanted to kiss her, she knew that she wasn't going to be able to run.

She finally came out of the bushes. 'I guess we can go back now.' She did not ever want to get back in that boat. She felt cold dread at the prospect. But she had no option, and she did not want to encourage any more of Jesse's particularly potent brand of empathy.

He scanned her face and nodded. She suspected that not a bit of her fear escaped him, but was rather warmed that he respected her enough not to say anything. She noticed how tanned his face had become. She noticed how the deep bronze of his skin made his eyes seem even greener, the green of water in a sheltered tropical cove. His hair was getting even more sun-streaked. And his lips were slightly chapped, sun-roughened, and she felt a shiver of desperation and longing when she looked at them.

She had to admit that she felt regret that he made no attempt to reopen negotiations for a kiss. She realised that some untamed part of her yearned to feel the firmness of his lips on hers. The boat seemed, suddenly, without danger. The danger seemed to lurk in some unknown thing within her.

He watched her as she rowed back. He liked what the sun had done to her complexion. It had lost that deathly pallor, and she looked healthy and sun-kissed.

He knew his guard was slipping. But then, maybe he had too much guard. It had been pointed out to him more than once that his secrecy about where he worked bordered on paranoia. Only Reggie knew. He remembered a poster he had once seen and chuckled. Just because you were paranoid, it didn't mean they weren't out to get you.

He looked at her again. Studied her with all his might. This one. Was she out to get him? Yes, it was true that the circumstances surrounding her arrival were strange, but after all, sometimes life was strange. And her name didn't seem not to fit her as it had before.

If she wanted something, she was not asking the right questions. He remembered Inge. The questions had never stopped. He had been so lost in the brownness of her big eyes that he had not ever recognised the shrewdness of the questions. He had flattered himself that she had been more interested in him than anybody had ever been before. He smiled grimly. Oh, sure. Your lover generally says, after you've related some highly personal anecdote, 'And what year was that, darling?'

All these years later the embarrassment of his own gullibility, his naïveté, still preyed on him. It was a game now. He had sworn that *they* would never get him again. And he was winning. They never had.

But for the first time he asked himself, at what price? How many truly nice people had his suspicion and cyncism turned him away from? Not many, he thought, remembering the woman in the green convertible—and then smiled at the habituation of his own cynicism. And at his own dishonesty. He was not truly concerned with whom he might have missed before.

He was concerned with missing this one. He could not unfasten his eyes from her. She was so unutterably lovely at times. Not her looks, though he had to admit that they were kind of growing on him, too. It was something else. The freshness of her; the flash of her smile across her mouth and in her eyes; the fine film of sweat that formed on her golden arms in the heat of the day; a kind of innocence of spirit that made him feel less jaundiced; her temper, beautiful and awesome, like a volcano erupting; the magnificent and desperate searching within herself; the almost tangible yearning to know who she was and how she fitted.

Finally, this afternoon, when he had seen that haunted and sad light in her eyes, he had come to believe that she was who she said she was. Just a lost soul looking for herself on the back-roads of British Columbia. He believed that. Believed it, and yet had no intention of telling her who he really was.

CHAPTER SIX

THE bank was an old one. The kind with a marble floor and high ceilings, the cashiers on tall stools behind a polished half-wall of walnut. A dull, stodgy place, that, like a library, inspired people to speak in confidential whispers.

And then the doors exploded open. And he stood there, long, hard legs braced apart. His body sending off a sizzle of tension. A navy blue bandanna covered his face to the bridge of his nose. His green eyes glinted above that. With warning, with something else. Roguish amusement, perhaps.

'This is a hold-up,' he said, his voice terse, and yet an iron calm running through it. He swept the sawn-off shotgun——

Sarah opened her eyes and glared at the bedroom ceiling. *'Dammit,'* she muttered. She couldn't picture Jesse holding a shotgun. She decided it wasn't loaded, and closed her eyes hopefully. No. She couldn't imagine him involved in a crime that required violence, even the subtle violence of terrifying people. Besides, bank robbers had no romance.

Lord, it was hot. She ran a hand through her sweat-tangled hair. Cursed the fact that the object of her mulling was probably fast asleep on the sofa. In the buff? Most likely. It was the only way to sleep in this cloying heat. Men like Jesse slept in the raw, anyway. Even if it was forty below.

Men like Jesse. Exactly what kind of man was that? She supposed she had put him in that rare category of men who exuded easy confidence in their bodies. So assured in their masculinity that there was nothing forced about the way they moved or talked or acted. They didn't throw their chests forward, swagger, talk roughly or loudly.

Even as debilitated as he was, with one arm strapped to his body, with a crutch as his constant companion, Jesse possessed an innate grace. A way of moving that was liquid. She, of course, possessed that same grace. But she had not come by hers naturally. Hers had been hammmered into her under her mother's vigilant and unceasing tutelage.

'Bien dans sa peau,' Sarah murmured. Comfortable in his own skin. She sat up suddenly, aware that these fevered thoughts were not likely to help her beat the heat, or sleep. She pulled a thin cotton T-shirt over her nakedness, and crept out of the room. The couch was empty. She went out on to the porch and gulped in the cool air coming off the lake. She started. She saw a light by the water. She relaxed. It was Jesse, with a book and a torch.

She hesitated. She imagined it was cooler by the water. But after the sizzling thoughts she'd just indulged in ... She shrugged them off, told herself it was the pull of the cool water she felt, not the pull of mysterious green eyes.

'Hi,' he said quietly, laying down the book. He smiled slowly, actually looked glad to see her.

'I couldn't sleep.'

'Hotter than Hades,' he agreed. 'Missing your air-conditioning?'

She sat down beside him, hugged her knees and looked out over the lake. It was cooler here. And infinitely beautiful, the moonbeam a luminous band of white woven through the black, velvet-soft water.

'No,' she said. 'Strangely enough, I'm not missing any of the amenities of city life.'

His smile deepened, softening the rugged features already softened somewhat by the moon. 'I've noticed you've made the adjustment to primitive with the ease of one born to a lack of luxury. It's really surprised me. Quite frankly, I thought you'd be crazy with boredom by now. And driving me crazy. You've been here more than a week, you know.'

'Have I?' She was genuinely surprised. Over a week had drifted by? As easily and naturally as the woolly white clouds drifted by on the endless blue of the summer sky?

'I think it would be impossible to be bored here,' she said thoughtfully. 'This cabin, this lake, these woods, the mountains. They're summer. They're everything summer is supposed to be and never was before.' She smiled softly. 'I never knew summer had a smell. And a feeling all its own. I don't know how to explain it, really, except it feels as if it's right inside me. Summer. It's slow and lazy and lovely.'

'You explained it just fine,' he said gruffly. 'Say, the moon's full. Do you feel like going for a row? Over to the island?'

There was a funny catch in his voice, and she turned her eyes to him. His eyes had captured some of the moon's cool silver. So had his lips. The sizzle re-entered the night.

'I told you. I'm never getting in that bucket again.' But that was only part of it. The other was that she did not want to be on that magical little island, on a magical night, with this mysterious, compelling man. The moon was too full. There was an invitation to surrender blissfully to madness on a night such as this. 'What are you reading?' she asked, trying to break the spell of the moon. It was too easy to remember what those lips had felt like, claiming her own. Too easy to desire to feel that again. But she was a woman accustomed to being pursued, and, since that afternoon on the island, Jesse had not pursued. He had acted as if he were sharing his cabin and his life with a younger brother. Sarah was unsure of the rules, when a woman felt desire and a man did not. She did not want to allow the moon to prod her into finding out.

Jesse picked up the book, and grinned. '*Tom Sawyer*. I feel slightly embarrassed to be admitting that.' He laughed. 'I'm still even reading it by flashlight.'

'Did you do that when you were a boy?' she asked with a smile. 'Read under your covers with a flashlight?'

'Nightly. I'm not sure that I had to, but it made it much more satisfying to think I was sneaking something. Did you do it, too? Read under the covers with a flashlight?'

She shook her head. 'No. I don't think I ever did anything even remotely naughty.'

'You must have missed all the fun of being a kid,' Jesse said softly.

'I was never really a kid,' she said, without much emotion.

'You can change that now, you know.'

'What?'

'Sure. You don't have to carry someone else's rules around for the rest of your life. You're all grown-up now, and you can make your own rules. You can let go of the control and the reserve. You can be spontaneous. You don't have to think it over before you laugh, before you speak, before you act. Actually, I think you are starting to make your own rules, aren't you?'

'I think so,' she agreed. 'It's hard, though. You see, Jesse, my whole life has been an appearance. My mother has always been concerned about how things appear. You want to *appear* to look this way and be that way, regardless of what you actually are. Appearances are everything. I do think how things look, before I act. That's second nature to me.'

His eyes were soft. 'That's very sad.'

She shrugged. 'My life hasn't been so bad.'

The look in his eyes intensified. 'After what you just told me, I'm beginning to suspect it was never your life. I'm beginning to understand all those fears of yours. I think it's people who don't risk who are really afraid. They're afraid the lights are going to get turned out before they've ever had a chance to see what it was all about. Before they've had their chance to dance with the stars and the sun and the moon.'

'Are you good at taking risks, Jesse?'

He looked thoughtful. 'A week ago, I would have said yes. In my line of work, you take a risk every time you——' He stopped abruptly, then continued. 'See? I take risks with my work, but not with people.'

'You still don't trust me.'

'I'm not sure who I don't trust.'

She sighed. He still didn't know who she was. Neither did she. Though sometimes, sometimes lately she was coming so much closer to knowing. Fragments of herself seemed to be brought into the light with each passing day. She was discovering what she liked to do, without looking for her mother's approval over her shoulder, without feeling Nelson's eyes on her back. It was for her, just for her. She was many things, and most of them darned wonderful, to her surprise and delight. And yet her discovery still had a fragmented quality, and she didn't know what it was going to take to melt everything together into a whole.

She stared out at the water, feeling a bleakness overlaying the magic of the moon. Love was a risk. Maybe the biggest one. Because there were never any guarantees that your emotion would be returned in kind. She had risked that particular risk. With Nelson. She had loved with her whole heart and soul. And not been loved in return. It left a hollow ache of hurt and wounded pride in the region of her heart.

But, suddenly, she wondered how she could feel that she had loved with her whole heart and soul when she only now seemed to be discovering what those were. She wondered if she had just played the role of love, like she had played all the other roles in her life. Because thinking of Nelson, now, did not do anything to her. She did not feel emptiness or sadness or even yearning for his company. He had been quite correct. He was an old man. Charming, but old, and his charm affected. She wondered why she hadn't seen it at the time. Because she had been so busy playing her own role, she hadn't had the time or the inclination to note that he was also just playing his?

Yes, the greatest risk was in loving, in trusting the care of your heart to another. She slanted a look at Jesse. Felt the physical pull of his moon-silvered eyes, and his sun-bronzed skin. But, no, she could not allow herself to risk loving Jesse. She could not. Because he would not trust, and she suspected that trust was the cornerstone of love. She wondered, a little frantically, why she would even think of him in terms of loving. Why? And then she wondered if she was already part-way there. And the terror of the risk rose up around her, and threatened to swallow her.

'Don't look so sad and shattered, Sarah,' he implored, the gentleness of his voice deepening the sensual timbre of it. 'Come here.'

Against her better judgement she moved close to him, and allowed him to circle her shoulders with his good arm. She felt suddenly safe, blissfully cool. She relaxed and closed her eyes.

> The police captain was burly and uni-formed, but his eyes held pride as he looked at the man in front of him. Every now and then a rookie would peer cautiously in the window of the office, his eyes filled with awe.
>
> 'Good work, James.'
>
> 'Thank you, sir,' Jesse said.
>
> 'You've broken the biggest organised crime-ring in the city. Unfortunately, that makes you a marked man.'
>
> Jesse smiled, that devil-may-care smile. That untamed smile. There were outlaws on both sides of the law, after all. Those men who were too independent to be captured by convention, men who had a thirst for danger, who excelled when they lived on the edge...
>
> 'I've got a place I can go,' Jesse stated quietly, 'until things cool down.'

Sarah felt sleepy peace. He was good. Of course

he was good. No criminal could possibly have the integrity of thought that was one of Jesse's hallmarks. No one who had hurt people, taken things which did not belong to them, could have Jesse's dignity. He was good. She knew he was good. And she slept.

She woke once. They were lying down now, her head nestled on his chest, his hand tangled in her hair. The breeze whispered peacefully over them. She slept. In the morning, she woke alone.

'Jesse, do you want pancakes for breakfast? Jesse?' The cabin was silent. She frowned. Went and looked through the rooms. No Jesse. She wondered where he had got to. Wandered into the bedroom. Her eyes caught on the cupboard door. It was unlocked.

'Jesse?' she called again. The cabin remained silent. She licked her lips, staring at the cupboard. She willed herself to walk away. This was his home, and whatever was behind those doors was his secret. For a moment, the peace she had felt sleeping in his arms returned. She felt certain that soon he would be ready. Soon, he would trust her. Damn! Her curiosity was burning within her, winning the battle between trusting him and finding out for herself. After all, he might never be ready to trust her, and she felt very ready to know all his secrets, right now.

She walked over, and touched the handle on the cupboard. Tried to pull her hand away, and couldn't. Darn it, all the lost sleep, and one little peep in this cupboard would tell her. Tell her what he did and why, and if he was the kind of a man a woman could risk her heart to. The thought astonished her. Was that what held her back from loving Jesse? Of course it was. A woman could not fall in love with a man who might be a villainous brute, who might make his living from causing others pain and suffering.

But, her heart scolded, if you love a man you must believe the best of him, without any evidence. You must trust.

Did she trust him? She supposed, in a way, she did. But she could trust him a lot more if she just *knew*. Besides, his only real worry was that she wouldn't be able to keep his secrets to herself. Well, she could do that, no matter how monstrous they were. She would never go running to the police. She couldn't rat on Jesse no matter what he did. And perhaps, if she had a piece of his mystery solved, a piece that he didn't know she had solved, she would know him better. Know how to touch that heart. How to——

She called his name once more and was answered by silence. Even as she despised herself, she swung open the cupboard door. She stared at the neat compartment within with astonishment. A desk was built into the wall, with shelves over it. The shelves overflowed with untidy papers. A word processor? But she had seen a generator outside this bedroom window. What on earth would he have a word processor for?

Her eyes caught on a stack of photos. Hesitating, she picked them up. Her eyes widened as she sifted through them, and a fist closed on her heart. There were hundreds of photos of women. All so different. Varying from studio shots to backyard snaps. Varying ages, from sixteen to sixty.

She felt sickened. Lord, what did Jesse do? Did he use his good looks to draw women to him, to romance them out of their hearts, their money? She had read about men who did that. Fatally charming, handsome men who preyed off loneliness and romantic minds and naïveté. Who made themselves so lovable and played their cruel games so well that sometimes their hapless victims still claimed to love them even after the awful truth was out.

Not Jesse! No, Jesse could not be like that! But what then of these photos? Lord, she was sorry she had opened this cupboard door. How could she even ask him what it meant? She felt a shimmer of fear. She stared at the rest of the papers, wondering, hoping, some answer, some innocent answer might lie here. She reached up——

'I think you've seen enough. Just close the door.'

She whirled round and stared at him. He was leaning in the door-frame, a tight smile on his face, his eyes cool and lethal.

'Jesse——'

'I thought, last night, that I had given you a fair chance. Thought that I had no reason not to trust you. Felt guilty that, after lecturing you on risk, I could not say that I had taken any chances, either, where you were concerned. But some vestige of caution remained. I gave you an opportunity to snoop, to pry.

'You know,' he said softly, something like sadness flitting momentarily through his eyes, 'a part of me actually prayed you wouldn't take it, Sarah. The part of me that has fallen in love with your eyes. I've never seen eyes like yours. They seem to be so much, to promise so much. Beautiful, beautiful eyes, that lie and lie and lie.' He shrugged. 'Close the cupboard door.'

She didn't. She picked up the photos desperately. 'Well, Lord knows you have enough eyes to compare mine to.' Her attempt to lighten the mood between them didn't work. His face was stone. 'Jesse, tell me about these. Please.' It was almost a whimper. She was begging him.

He brushed by her, tore the photos out of her hand and slammed them back on the desk top. 'No.' He put a hand on her shoulder and pushed her abruptly out of his way. He slammed the cupboard door, padlocking it shut with a snap. He whirled round and looked at her. 'What were you looking for?' he demanded, his eyes snapping, his voice a hiss.

'I don't know, Jesse,' she stumbled. 'A clue, I guess. A clue to you.' A tear slithered down her cheek.

'Forget the tears, lady. I'm unmoved. You've already admitted you're rather good at putting on appearances.'

She stared at him with disbelieving hurt. An unspeakable cruelty had entered his eyes. And he was using her own words, the words she had *risked* telling him, to cut her to ribbons.

She wanted nothing more than to turn and flee from the savage indictment in his eyes. But, with what little bravery she had left, she tried to redeem herself in his eyes.

'Jesse, I never put on appearances for you. At least, not that I was aware of. I think,' she continued softly, 'that you're the very first person I didn't feel I had to pretend for.'

He snorted with disbelief and disgust. 'Sarah, you're standing here with your damn fingers in the pie. It really is the wrong time to convince me of how honourable you are. I don't appreciate being played for a fool.'

'I'm ashamed of looking through your things,' she admitted softly. 'I am. Jesse, can't you just see it as what it was? I'm human. I wanted to know what dark secrets you had locked within you. I wanted to know about the dark world you inhabit.'

'The dark world I inhabit?' His voice was surprised, but sneering too. 'What the hell are you talking about?'

She took a deep breath. 'Jesse, I know. I know you do something that's on the other side of the law. I know you're on the run. I know you might be involved with the Mafia.' She yearned for the certainty that she had felt last night that he was good. But his eyes were so hard and cold, his face so unyielding that he was a stranger again. Yes, a dangerous and frightening stranger.

His look was measuring—for a moment he seemed to waver. In that moment, she glimpsed again something of his goodness and her willingness to believe in him rose, only to be dashed when he shook his head savagely. His voice was harsh when he spoke.

'I don't believe your eyes any more. I won't. Don't stand there looking at me with wide-eyed innocence, concocting a tale only a fool would believe, and laughing at me because I'm halfway on my way to believing it. You should be an actress, you know that? Lord, you play this game well. And cruelly. Whoever you work for has found themselves a real prize. You can tell them that. At the same time, you can tell them you drew a blank on Jesse James.' A light dawned in his eyes. 'I get it. Jesse James. You've had your excuse to pry through my life ready since the moment you arrived, haven't you? It's clever, in a despicable sort of way, Sarah, I grant you that.'

'I don't work for anybody,' she denied. 'And I know it sounds far-fetched. When you say it out loud it does. But it didn't seem——' she faltered, trying to figure out how to tell him about her father's description of this area in a few succinct phrases.

He didn't give her the opportunity. His eyes were flat and cold on her face. 'Even if that were true, which I severely doubt, I wouldn't be very flattered by it.'

'Then how do you explain those pictures?'

'I have no intention of explaining those pictures, or anything else about my life to you. I don't owe you explanations for puzzles that resulted from a blatant invasion of my privacy.'

'Jesse——'

He took a step towards her, and looked at her with menace flashing in his eyes. 'Don't call me Jesse any more,' he said roughly. 'I don't find your game amusing. Let's just forget the ruse. I am sick of it. Do you understand? Call me by my real name.'

'Jacoby?' she ventured uncertainly.

'I told you, I'm not playing. But you keep on playing if you want. All by yourself.'

He whirled away from her and slammed out of the room. She stood staring at the empty doorway for a long time, tears slithering down her cheeks. So his name was not Jacoby, either. Just as she had always suspected. But what was his real name, and why was he so certain it was a secret she already knew?

And why did she feel this inside? This self-disgust as if she'd betrayed her only friend in the world? Why did she think of him as a friend?

Because, she acknowledged softly, he had seen her. Always. He had been the only man in her memory that had not fallen for her face, her figure, her glamour, her status. From the very beginning, he had seen something else. She suspected that he had seen whatever it was she always wanted others to see, only they never had.

'The part of me that has fallen in love with your eyes,' he'd said. Her tears gathered strength. She fell on to the bed and wept. So he had been feeling it, too, this strange pull from within. The power of that mysterious force called love. He had been feeling it, too, and she had destroyed it by not trusting him, by her childish need to know more about him than he was willing to reveal.

She ached with loss. She had not known exactly how strongly she felt about Jesse until this moment when she knew she had lost him.

CHAPTER SEVEN

SARAH sipped her coffee glumly, and stared out of the window. The morning sun was just now touching the lake, creating an illusion of thousands of star sapphires out there winking brightly. She sighed. How dared it be such a beautiful day again, when she was feeling so bleak?

Jesse had not spoken to her for several days. Now and then she would feel his eyes, icy and accusing, resting on her. She looked a little deeper and thought she saw more there—the pain of betrayal. She had tried several times to talk to him. He had taken to disappearing for the day, leaving the cabin early in the morning, not coming back till late at night.

She looked blackly at the bright, brilliant summer day. Where was the rain? Rain of the force and intensity that had heralded her arrival here? Damn it, that would force him to stay inside. She was worried about him. How was he managing to eat? Look after his arm? Bathe? Shave? Yes, a few rain-bound days were what they needed. To get these feelings out in the open. To find answers for all the unasked questions on both sides.

She knew he wouldn't be able to resist her, if she could just get him in her clutches for a few days. She knew it, because she knew he cared about her.

Below that slow, bubbling anger, he still cared. Otherwise, she wouldn't still be sitting here. Otherwise, he would have sent her packing down that long and lonely road with no regard for what would happen to her. For, as angry as he was, he had not suggested her leaving. She wondered if the flicker of hope that that made her feel was naïve.

What did he have all those pictures for? She refused to think about it, rising abruptly from her sunshiny nook and slamming her empty coffee-cup into the sink. She had been over that particular question about ten thousand times in her mind. Could not come up with a satisfactory explanation. Had realised, anyway, how incredibly futile it was to try and imagine what Jesse was up to. He was going to have to tell her. She was going to have to make him tell her. And she didn't have a clue how she was going to do that.

She went and picked up her drawing materials, drifted out into the sun, and walked along the rocky shore of the beach. After a while she settled down, and gazed at the lake. She made a few tentative strokes on the paper, ripped the sheet out of the book and crumpled it. She flipped through the pages of her book, stopped and sighed. It called her. This one work called her, and she could not resist its call.

Except for her sketch of the apple tree, most of her sketches had been quick and casual. She could complete half a dozen of them in a day. Not so with this one. She looked down at the strong profile beginning to take shape, and sighed. It was taking forever. And yet each line came out of her, thoughtful and perfect. And it was him, even though all that was there were a few beginning lines. The strength and grace and pride were emerging from the bold strokes of her charcoal.

She closed her eyes for a moment, calling up what she wanted in her mind's eye. This was going to be the hardest part. His eyes. How could one possibly capture such eyes? And yet not to capture the eyes would be not to capture him. They came to her, exactly as she wanted them. She could picture them. Mysterious. Unfathomable. A trace of hard suspicion. A trace of glowing laughter. A trace of something else that she couldn't put her finger on. She opened her eyes, and stared at her drawing.

The tension rose in her, and she put the drawing pad aside. She couldn't do it right now. It wasn't that she didn't feel like it—it was that fine tension, as if she was being watched. Where was he? Was he watching her?

Her eyes caught on the island and she remembered the brief tranquillity she had known there, and felt an unbearable yearning. She knew, suddenly, that if she went there she would be able to draw him. Knew it. She looked at the boat, and smiled with relief at the complete lack of trepidation she felt. She got up, ambled over, threw in the pad, and strapped on a life-jacket.

Within minutes she was skimming rather gracelessly over the surface of the lake, feeling the heat of the reflected sun flow into her bones and calm her. The shore grew more distant and her tension seemed to have been left back there.

Ah, and there he was now—her tension, Jesse, suddenly appeared on the bank she had left behind. He waved at her.

Waved? It was terribly tempting to go back and see what change had occurred in him that would cause such a friendly gesture. But no, he was probably just trying to lure her back so that he could tell her to get out of *his* boat. Or maybe he wanted to come to the island. Well, that was out of the question. She needed a day completely away from him, from his frowning silences, from the contempt that rose in his eyes every time he looked at her. She raised her hand back to him, acknowledging him, nothing more, and moved on.

His shouted 'Sarah' drifted, muffled by distance, across the water. He shouted something else. She couldn't hear him. She ignored him. Saw his arm fall to his side. She couldn't see his expression, but she could tell by his stance that there was still a tension in him. A tension she didn't want to be around today.

He stood watching her row away, the feeling of impotent anger growing with each determined stroke of her oar.

'Why should I care?' he muttered out loud, thinking of the storm warning he had just heard over the radio. But, dammit, he did care. As much as he wanted not to, he still cared about the traitorous vixen. He could tell from the hurt look on her face that she thought all this rage was directed at her. It wasn't. But it should have been, so it wouldn't hurt to let her think that.

No, the rage was directed at himself. Because, after all the years and all the lessons, he still seemed to be attracted to the very same kind of woman. This time she was a panther, not a kitten, but still the same crafty, untrustworthy nature.

Or was he making too much of that, too? He squinted once more after the boat, sighed and turned away. In truth, he'd felt like a bit of a creep setting up a trap like that. She had walked into the trap and it had given him a kind of grim satisfaction. But maybe what she had said was true. Maybe she was only human, curious. He knew that his very bent towards secrecy ignited curiosity in people. What made him seem even angrier yet, was this: if the tables were turned, if it had been she who held the secrets and left the door unlocked, would he have looked?

No way, he thought righteously. But a part of him doubted. Curiosity was what propelled him through life. Solving the mysteries of people was how he made his living. Would he have walked away from the solution to a puzzle? Had he ever?

He stopped, before entering the cabin, and looked once more at the tiny dot of a boat forging across the water. He scanned the sky. Crystal-clear. Perhaps the storm would miss here. His eyes returned to the boat, and he felt his stomach twist protectively. He thought it would be very nice if one could order caring to stop, shut it off as easily as you shut off a light. The anger, at his own lack of control, started up again. He turned and stamped into the house.

She was at the island before she realised she had got there without a trace of fear. She had been so thoroughly wrapped up in her appreciation of the day, and her thoughts of the portrait of Jesse, that she simply had not remembered the fact that the boat could tip. Only if she'd been fool enough to stand up, she thought with a trace of mirth as she tugged the boat up onshore. It wasn't as if a tiny lake like this could really get the tidal waves of her imagination.

She walked around to the other side of the small island, wanting her isolation to be complete, not wanting to feel as if prying eyes were fastened on her. She picked up her pad, and a piece of charcoal. Her brow furrowed in concentration, her mind oddly blank, save for the picture she was trying to capture, she went to work.

She didn't know how long she worked at it. Hours? Perhaps. She was suddenly aware that her body had been held still for so long that it ached. She gave her hand a rueful shake, trying to relieve the cramping of her fingers. And then that was forgotten.

She stared at the drawing with wonder and awe. She had done this. She wasn't quite sure how. But he was there. Not just the lines of his face, but his spirit and his soul, captured on paper. She sighed, suddenly exhausted, with a sense of satisfaction and contentment. He could not take this. His business acquaintance should be here any day. She had seen him watching the road, cocking his ear at the least sound, knew he was waiting to be rescued. From her. Knew she would be disposed of with not so much as a backward glance. She had nothing of Jesse to keep, to hold to herself, to weep over. Now she did. She had this.

She closed her eyes. They were stinging from straining them for so long. Where would she go next? To her father's, as planned, she supposed. It suddenly occurred to her that she no longer *had* to see her father. She wanted to, but she didn't feel driven as she had at the beginning of this detoured journey.

Because, she realised, she knew the truth now. Her father could not tell her who Sarah Moore was. Not any more than her mother had been able to. She had to answer that question for herself. She laid her palm across her drawing. And she had. In the last few weeks, she had answered it herself. It was not something that had words. She could not make a list of adjectives that would sum it up. It was this feeling inside her. The feeling of almost wholeness. The child and the woman coming together. It was the feeling that had allowed her to step into that boat again, the feeling that was growing so strong within her that the fearful thoughts that had haunted her all her life had not been present at all in the last week. She had even started to use the lighter to light the stove in the chill of the morning. She didn't eat off the plates with caution any more.

It was so strong, this winged thing inside her, that not even Jesse's silent and constant disapproval could shake it or shatter it. Jesse thought she was something that she knew she was not. It wasn't that his opinion didn't matter to her—it was just that she could not allow his opinion to shape her reality, as her mother's opinions had shaped her reality. As Nelson's opinions had shaped her reality. As she had been determined to let her father's opinions shape her reality. Until she had ended up here. Now she knew that all her life she had placed others in charge of her own destiny, placed others in charge of what she felt about herself, and that was over.

No, her reality, the soul of Sarah Moore, was safe and strong within her. With a smile of contentment, giving herself the hug she had never received as a child, she let the weariness take her, peacefully, into the land of sleep.

A raindrop awoke her. She struggled awake, her first thought for the picture at her side. It had not been raining long enough to damage it. She closed the cover on her book and shoved it under her sweater. It was then that her eyes caught on the lake and her mouth went slack with shock.

Could this raging water be the innocent lake she had crossed this morning? The water had gone from sparkling blue to ominous black, the black contrasting sharply with the foamed white-caps that hissed on top of the waves.

She felt a flash of fear that was quickly displaced by this new calm that she knew to be at the centre of herself. Well, so what? She was safe, and she didn't have to attempt to go back to the cabin until the weather let up. She forced away the thought that it might be a week before that happened. She felt annoyed. She'd been praying for this storm for days, and now that it had finally arrived she wasn't going to be able to take advantage of Jesse's forced nearness. Stupid island, she thought, forgetting every bit of affection she'd felt for it only hours ago.

Sarah got up, brushed herself off, and then crossed back over to the other side of the island. She squinted across the water at the cabin. She could barely see it for the rain, now slashing down in grey waves. Drat, she was willing to bet that he had it warm and cosy in there. And, no doubt, he'd be delighting in the fact that he had it all to himself, that he wouldn't have to be fending off her attempts to negotiate a peace, to negotiate something more than a peace.

Her heart suddenly caught in her throat. Lord, what was that? She squinted, uneasily, wanting to disbelieve. But no, there was a boat out there. The bright green canoe that had lain so innocently beside the rowing-boat this morning. And that hunched frame in it had to be Jesse.

Why? Why was he out there? And how was he managing to control the canoe at all, with his one arm useless to him? Her breath began to come in ragged gasps as she watched the canoe being tossed on the rough water.

Bloody fool, she thought. But she didn't hesitate. She was running towards the boat, the fear gone, replaced with the energy of purpose. She got in, incredulous at how the rough water made her small craft so hard to manipulate, so hard to move. But her heart was set in a stubborn course, and that lent her a power she wouldn't have believed she had. She made her agonising way out into the open lake, towards him.

She could hear him shouting, his words lost on the wind. Not quite lost. He was telling her to go back, in the most unflattering terms. She ignored him.

It seemed like hours before she approached the canoe. 'Throw me the rope,' she yelled at Jesse.

He glared at her, and for a moment she thought he was going to be stubborn enough to ignore her command. But then he threw her the rope.

Remembering the lesson about the balance of the rowing-boat, she stayed low while she crept forward, pulled the rope in so that his vessel was close to hers, and lashed it solidly in place.

Then she went back to the seat, her arms screaming in agony, and rowed back towards the island. She could see Jesse huddled in the canoe, his face white with pain, holding his arm to his side. The sling was gone, she noted. Damn men! How could they be so stupid and stubborn, and expect to survive into their old age? And when had she started to care so much if he survived into his old age, anyway?

Always.

Finally she got the boats into the shallow water, jumped out into water up to her knees, and pulled them up on to shore.

Jesse got awkwardly out of the canoe, still cradling his injured arm against him. He came up behind her, his good hand grasping her shoulder with hurtful force and spinning her around.

'Bloody fool,' he hissed, his eyes killing.

'Me?' she shouted. 'Me? You pompous ass! It wasn't me out there in the middle of the storm, with a broken arm and a wobbly boat. What the hell did you think you were doing?' It was only after the angry words had come rushing out of her that she really looked into his face. His eyes were hollowed with pain, his face washed with a sickly grey pallor. She reached up and touched his face with a tenderness that erased the harshness of her words.

'Oh, Jesse,' she whispered.

His hand tangled in her hair, and he pulled her roughly towards him. His kiss was savage and punishing. Finally, she knew he was releasing the anger, the frustration, the hurt. And what a way to release it. And she welcomed that release, and sensed the moment that he had released it all. Because the kiss changed, melting into tender hunger, being gentled by the long-suppressed yearning he was now surrendering to.

'We're getting very wet,' she murmured into his ear.

He shoved her abruptly away from him, stood staring at her. 'Didn't you hear me calling you this morning?'

'Yes.'

'Well, why didn't you come back?'

'I didn't want to.'

A slight grin tugged at the harsh line of his lips and was gone. 'You impudent woman. Didn't want to! I had just heard a storm warning on the radio. I was trying to get you to come back. And then I kept an onshore vigil most of the day, waiting for you to notice the clouds gathering and get yourself back across that lake. What were you doing, for crying out loud?'

'Sleeping.'

'Sleeping,' he repeated incredulously.

'Jesse, why did you come? What were you thinking of? With your arm——'

'I was thinking of you. I was thinking that you might try to come across again in the storm. As soon as the rain started, I knew I had to come. I hoped I could beat the storm. I wasn't counting on being so slowed up by this——' he winced as he moved the arm.

'Jesse, I still don't understand——'

He turned away from her, but not before she saw an anguished light dance briefly across his eyes. 'I was worried about you,' he admitted gruffly. 'You don't have a whole lot of common sense. I mean, what was a girl from New York going to do if the weather set in for a week? Would you stay here and starve? Would you know how to build a lean-to? Would you try and get the boat back across?' His voice had a funny catch in it. 'Would you be afraid and lonely?'

'Oh, Jesse,' she whispered.

'I don't know if I would have bothered,' he said defensively, 'except I came across something of yours this morning. Before you say anything, I know. It's a double standard. I didn't want you snooping through my stuff, but I sure as hell looked through yours at the first opportunity. I'm sorry. It's as if I couldn't stop myself. It made me understand a bit why you went into that cupboard when I'd asked you not to.'

'I don't have anything for you to see,' she pointed out with puzzlement.

'I found your drawings.'

She glared at him. 'Came across them, Jesse? They were under the bed!'

He had the decency to look a tiny bit sheepish. 'Yes, I know.' His eyes locked on hers. 'Sarah, they're beautiful. Incredible. I felt as if I saw you. In every one of them. No, not in one of them. But the one of the apple tree...' his voice trailed off. 'You are one beautiful, beautiful woman.'

She blushed under the intensity of his gaze. 'It's a very good thing you feel that way,' she said lightly, 'because I think you're marooned with me.'

He nodded, his eyes left her face, and he studied the lake. 'That brings us to the point at hand. I think we should stay here, at least until the weather lets up. I brought a tent, and food and dry clothes, just in case that's what we decided to do.'

She made him sit under the relative dryness of some trees, while she listened to his instructions about setting up a camp. Within a short while she had managed to get the tent up. They sat inside, a fire not far away, the smell of perking coffee and bubbling stew mingling with the scent of the wet earth. She was glad they had decided to stay on the island. It felt like a bit of an adventure, this roughing it, this learning to co-exist with the elements.

They drank the warming coffee and ate the stew in companionable silence. Finally, his hand touched hers. 'Sarah, I'm sorry. When I looked at those drawings, I knew I'd been a complete fool. Everything you are is in them. They are so completely honest, so fresh, so innocent. I'm sorry. What I saw in your eyes was true, all along. Maybe I over-reacted, because I wanted to push you away, because I'm a little frightened of the things I'm starting to feel for you.'

She digested that, reached for his hand and gave it a hard squeeze. 'Thank you.' For two things: for trusting her, and for having the guts to admit he'd been wrong. It suddenly seemed too intense between them and she took her hand from his. 'So, which drawing didn't you like?'

He looked at her, a frown creasing his forehead. 'The one that looked like you, but wasn't. You called it Sahara. I thought that was appropriate. She was a wasteland. Beautiful, but empty somehow. I can't explain it. As I say, she looked vaguely like you, and not like you at all.'

'Thank you,' Sarah said softly. She was thankful, too, that he obviously didn't make any connection between a drawing called Sahara and the missing model they'd heard about on the radio with a very similar name.

'Who is she? Your sister?'

Sarah smiled, a tiny, slightly sad smile. 'Just somebody I used to know. I don't know her any more. The likeness is a coincidence.'

His lips were suddenly buried in her hair, trailing fiery kisses down the nape of her neck. His lips moved up and captured her mouth, and the storm invaded the sanctuary of their tent. Heated. Electrical. Raging. And yet soothing.

She met his lips, met his energy and passion with all of her own. It was time. It was time for the woman and the child to meet.

'Are you sure?' he whispered huskily as she unclasped the buckle on his belt.

'Very sure,' she said. She didn't know how she could be so sure. She had had the opportunity to do this many times. And her own uncertainty had always stopped her. Her mother had encouraged her. A tasteful affair with a well-known celebrity couldn't have harmed her career at all. But this part of herself did not belong to her mother. And she realised that it had not belonged to Sahara, either. This part of herself belonged to Sarah. And, in a different way, this part of herself, this outlaw part of herself, belonged to the man who lay beside her, his mouth tangled in hers, his hand caressing with sweet passion.

'Ouch.' He cursed. 'I don't know how we're going to do this, Sarah.'

She smiled at him gently, lowered her lips to his. 'We'll think of something,' she murmured.

And they did.

CHAPTER EIGHT

IT continued to rain. For one day and then two. A few times the weather broke for long enough that they could have made a dash across the lake, if they were so inclined. Neither of them was so inclined.

The island was a magic place, even more set apart from the world than the isolated cabin. Modern life had not touched this small oasis at all. If the cabin had been rustic, the island really was primitive. No lights, no stove, no books, no radio. And yet, it lacked absolutely nothing. Simplicity reigned. Simplicity and enchantment. A better place for new lovers to get to know each other had never been created. The island allowed them their intensity, their intimacy, without interruptions, without pressures, without demands, without a deadline to bring them back to the real world.

They made love until Jesse started to complain that he was probably going to be crippled for life, and then would add with a wry grin that it was worth it. They shared the island with a shy deer, who grew bolder and bolder until often they sat together, in the rain, watching and being watched back. Sarah held grass, sitting motionless forever... until finally she was rewarded when the deer came and took the grass from her hand.

She had never talked with another human being as she talked to Jesse. That was part of the island's magic. There was simply nothing to come between them. No pressures. No doubts. They talked and laughed and played. They were children. And they were very, very grown-up.

'Are you ever going to tell me what you do, Jesse?' she asked one night, languishing in the comfort of his arm around her, the hardness of his chest beneath her back.

He nuzzled her hair. 'Not yet. Please, not yet.'

'Why? Is it so terrible?'

He laughed. 'Some people probably would think it was a crime that I make so much money doing what I do. Could we leave it though, Sarah, for now?'

'But you are going to tell me? Jesse, I want to know you. All of you. And there seems to be this big secret between us. Surely, now, you trust me.'

'Nope. Never met a woman I could trust.'

He was teasing and she smacked him smartly. 'That's because you have admitted an attraction to women who were kittenish and coy—and simply awful. I cannot imagine you with women like that.'

He laughed huskily, looked at her with tender wonder. 'Me neither. Not now. Imagine going back to a kitten after you've had a panther.' He wrapped his hand in her thick dark hair. 'A beautiful black panther, with grace and strength, and——' his voice lowered to a growl '—appetite.'

'Jesse, please quit trying to change the subject. Tell me who you are.'

'Don't you know?' he asked, a faint hurt in his voice, in his magnificent green eyes.

She sighed, and smiled. 'Yes, I guess I know. But still——'

'Sarah, when we cross back over, I'll fling open the doors of that cupboard and you can rummage around in it to your heart's content. You'll find out everything there is to know about me in there. But for now, just for a while longer, could you give me this gift? This gift of being liked and appreciated for what I am and not for what I do? It's been a long, long time since anybody has looked at me uninfluenced by their prejudices. It's been a long time since a woman looked at me who didn't want something from me more than myself.'

'Could you just tell me one thing?'

'OK, one.'

'Are you an outlaw, Jesse?'

He started to laugh. 'Jesse James, eh?' he teased. He looked at her face, and became more serious. 'That's a funny word, an archaic word,' he finally said thoughtfully. 'I mean, outlaws aren't real, any more. They're the stuff of legend, the years acting like heatwaves rising off hot pavement. What's real and what's illusion? Was there really romance and daring and rough justice in their lifestyles? I guess that not really knowing all the details of their stories and their motivations is part of the appeal, part of the mystery, part of what makes history treat them fairly gently.'

She smiled to herself. 'I think the word suits you more than ever.'

'Do you? I'm kind of flattered, actually, though I don't know why. I guess it's flattering to have a beautiful woman see you as rugged and bold, and mysterious and dashing.' He arched a villainous eyebrow playfully at her. Then he leaned forward, deadly serious and earnest. 'I like people with an imagination. I'm glad you have one. I'm glad you still believe in outlaws.'

'I never thought of myself as having much imagination,' she confided in him.

'How could you draw all the time and say you don't have imagination?'

'I didn't draw all the time. Not until I came up here. I haven't drawn since I was a little girl.'

'Why?' When she shrugged, he frowned. 'See, you have your mystery, too, don't you, Sarah? Some day, maybe you'll trust me enough to tell me about what made you such a different little girl.'

'I trust you enough to tell you right now,' she said solemnly. 'But I don't want to. I don't want anything to touch us here. Not anything sad, anyway. I'm just starting to understand how sad my childhood was. And I will tell you about it some day. I want to. But I liked your idea of being liked and appreciated in this moment, for no reason at all. Not because we've earned it, or need sympathy, or have a fascinating past, but simply because we are.'

'Would it be breaking those lovely rules to get a peek at that sketch pad you've been hauling around here?'

'If you promise loud oohs and ahs,' she directed him with a grin. But when she sat down beside him with her sketch pad, she had grown very serious. 'I really am glad you wanted to see this. Because I've really wanted to show it to you. It's a part of me. One of the best parts of me.'

He went through it slowly, pulling her under the weight of his arm so that she could flip pages, and he could point out the things that really grabbed his attention. She was amazed by his insight. Without fail, he saw the heart of each of her drawings, commented on just the thing that she had been trying to express.

'You're very, very good,' he said softly. 'These are very much like the other ones. There is a piece of you shining out of each one. It's as if I can see a little glimpse of your soul, Sarah. It's incredible.'

She came to the page with the drawing of him on it, and tried to flip by it before he could get a good look. But his hand stopped her, and he stared at the picture, his very stillness making her feel threatened. She could sense the heat rising in her cheeks, and she tried again to change to a different page.

'Don't,' he commanded softly. Finally, his eyes found hers. He shook his head slowly, ran his hand through the silk of his hair, and then looked back to the drawing. 'Lord, Sarah.'

'You don't like it,' she stated, with flat hurt.

'Like it? I like it so much it makes me feel vulnerable. I feel as if it's suddenly my soul we're looking into, and I wasn't prepared for that. I thought we'd be looking at your drawings, so we'd see *your* soul. Not mine. How did you do this? How did you see this?'

'I don't know,' she said simply.

His green gaze locked on hers. 'Sarah,' he said softly. 'You have captured me.' He buried his face in her hair. 'Oh, lord, woman, you have captured me. In more ways than one.'

Sarah woke and stretched sensuously the next morning. It had been better than it had ever been. It had moved beyond the physical. A joining of two great and proud spirits. She found the beauty of it slightly terrifying. It opened her, left her vulnerable and shaken.

She was aware of a tingling contentment that saturated her whole body. The full glory of being a woman welled up within her. She was aware, suddenly, of the price-tag this glory might have. The potential for pain/ in having given so totally to another human being. She reached for Jesse, needing the reassurance of his satiny flesh, of his green gaze resting on her with such pleasure, such wonder.

Jesse was gone. A sudden unnamed fear pierced her contentment. Lord, what was she thinking? What was she doing? She remembered that stack of photos. She knew nothning about this man—by his choice, she knew nothing about him. Last night had been such a tender adventure, but where had the words been? There had been no words of love, of commitment.

She untangled herself from the twisted sleeping-bag, pulled on a rumpled shirt, scooted from the tent.

Jesse stood at the water's edge, gazing towards the cabin. He turned and looked at her, a smile dancing across his face, lighting up his eyes. Her fear dissipated. He had promised her that all the questions would be answered. In time they would be.

'Morning, gorgeous.' She went to him, nestled herself under his arm. It tightened around her.

He nodded towards the cabin. 'We've got company.'

She jerked her head in that direction. She could see the sun glinting off a silver-grey car. 'Your friend,' she said woodenly, the nameless dread intensifying in her.

He chuckled, without mirth. 'Reggie and I are many things, though I don't think friendship is ever a word that has entered into our relationship.'

No, that wasn't quite true, he amended mentally. Once, when he'd been very young, he'd thought Reggie was his friend. Between Reggie and Karen he'd been talked into going on Bobby Carlton's late-night show. It had been against his every instinct, against his soul-deep need for privacy, solitude.

'I don't want people to know who I am,' he'd said. 'I like anonymity. I like being able to go out for walks without being mobbed, to go and buy toothpaste at the corner store.'

Karen had looked pained. Karen had liked fame—the more the better. Reggie had laughed loudly, slapped his knee a few times. 'Ye gads, boy. You think you're Elvis Presley, or what? People pay attention to rock stars. They mob movie stars. You can rest easy about buying your toothpaste.'

So, he'd agreed. Partly because he had still felt that he could make Karen happy, and partly because Reggie had made him feel as if he'd been foolish and egotistical to imagine that anybody was going to pay any attention to him.

He had been mobbed by near-hysterical women outside the stage door after the show. Later, he had found out that Reggie had hired the entire mob of out-of-work actresses. It had started the whole ball rolling. All that had been needed was the suggestion that he was unbearably sexy, and American women ate it up. He could no longer buy his own toothpaste. He had worked very hard at sinking back into blessed oblivion, but if anything that had seemed to whet the appetites of the gossip-magazine crowds even more. For a while he'd wandered, unsuspecting, into well-laid traps. Not for years, though, not since he'd honed his skill at the game. Yes, three years since the last time a picture had appeared of him anywhere. Three years, and still, occasionally, that light of recognition that he dreaded so much, lighting up in a stranger's eyes. 'Say, aren't you...?'

No, Reggie was not his friend. But he was as ruthless as a rattlesnake when it came to driving a bargain, and he was no longer dealing with a twenty-five-year-old kid. Yes, there had been a not so subtle change in who the boss was after that incident. Reggie minded his place. With argument. And woefully. But he could be trusted to stay in line.

She felt that apprehension creep up her spine again at the chill in Jesse's voice when he spoke of his visitor across that water. What did she know of this tall, lean man who stood beside her? Who had shown her a side of exquisite gentleness last night that had been delightful and surprising, but had never shown her anything else of himself?

No, she told herself staunchly. That simply wasn't true. Everything he did was a reflection of himself. The way he spoke, and the way he walked, and moved, and the way he caressed her in the deepness of the night. All of this was Jesse.

His eyes were on her face. 'It's over, Sarah. We're not stuck with one another any more.'

Her early morning doubts came back with a rush—enfolded her like a misty cloud of dreariness and desperation. She struggled against the tears that ached behind her eyes. So, for him it had been a fling. Taking advantage of an opportunity that had presented itself. Nothing more. What a fool she was. She should have at least said the words she was feeling, and seen how he reacted to them being spoken out loud. Perhaps she could have saved herself some heartache by saying the words 'I love you'. Jesse probably would have managed to get that boat back across the lake then—even if a full-fledged blizzard was blowing over the lake.

She turned from him, and began to furiously rip apart the camp, stuffing the tent and pegs into the bag. He came up behind her.

'Do you think you might like to stay?'

She whirled round and looked at him, afraid that her love was in her eyes. 'What?'

'Stay.' He looked almost shy. 'For the rest of the summer. We'll go into town. I'll get checked over by a doctor. You can pick up some duds. Then we'll come back.'

She wanted to weep with her confusion. She didn't know what she wanted. But she did know what she didn't want—she didn't want to be some summer fling, a dalliance to keep his mind off the work he wanted so badly to be doing.

'I just don't know what I want, Jesse.'

His face closed. 'OK. Think about it. I guess I was starting to think you liked it here.'

How could men be so obtuse? Yes, she liked it here. Yes, she liked him. So much. She felt such a passion for both this place and this man. Passion that would grow over the summer, and then what? He'd wish her a casual goodbye and good luck with her life? Wouldn't it be easier to say the goodbyes and the good lucks now?

She was aware of Jesse watching her face as she rowed back over the glass surface of the lake towards the cabin. She tried to keep it impassive. She didn't know what she was going to do. It would hurt so much to say goodbye to him now. Who was she to say that it would hurt worse in a few months? What if she took a chance, stayed, lived it moment by moment? Took each day as a gift, a gift in loving, and asked no more? Did not ask that the future be guaranteed for her? Did not try and peer into the crystal ball of tomorrow? She suspected that if she said goodbye today, that if she did not take that chance, it would be over. That she would never see Jesse again. But if she waited, perhaps there was a chance that he would begin to love her as she loved him. That at the end of the summer he could not let her go, would not want to, ever. It did not even seem like a choice, really.

Except, she thought again, of how little she knew about the man sitting across from her. What about those pictures? What about his shadowy other life?

Well, what about them, she demanded of herself? And suddenly she knew the truth. It didn't matter what Jesse was doing. She loved him. She trusted a basic integrity she had seen about him. What he did could not change who he was.

He had risked something of himself by asking her to stay. Now was it her turn? To risk? To risk loving without knowing what she would get in return?

'Jesse, I'll stay.' She laughed as he stood up, crouching. 'Jesse, sit down ... you're going to tip the boat ... for heaven's sake, Jesse, get back on your seat ... Jesse——'

He was beside her and she slid over. He took one oar with his good hand, nibbled at her ear. 'I'm so glad. We have so much to talk about. So much to learn from one another.'

'Jesse,' she giggled. They were going in a circle. 'You're rocking the boat.'

'Then row, woman,' he teased, continuing his assault on her ear.

She put down the oar, wrapped her arms around his neck and kissed him thoroughly. She picked up the oar, looked into his eyes, now dazed by longing. 'Row,' she ordered. He sighed.

There was no sign of life when they approached the other shore. 'Your friend must have gone exploring.'

'No, Reggie's not exactly the outdoors type. He's not exploring. He's ripping the house apart looking for a drink.'

Sarah cast Jesse a glance. So, it was a less than savoury type who had come to visit. What was Jesse's business with this man? What was Jesse's business? She would know, soon. He had said he would fling open that cupboard door. Did she really want to know, any more?

They walked up to the cabin. She stopped and looked at the car. It was huge and sleek and grey. Ominous, somehow, like the car a gangster drove.

Her heart was fluttering nervously in her throat when they went to the door. She felt instant relief. The man who sat sulkily at the kitchen nook did not look like a gangster. He looked like a tourist, and a very tacky one at that. He was wearing a straw hat with a loud coloured band around it. His shirt shouted. He had bermuda shorts on that clashed, and knee socks pulled up tight over his fat legs.

Despite the fact that he looked harmless enough, Sarah hung back cautiously in the shadow of the porch. She wanted to see how this man and Jesse reacted towards each other.

He looked at Jesse. 'Hell's bells, what did you do to your arm? When? You're off schedule, aren't you?'

Jesse didn't even answer. He was given no room.

'What's going on? I sat in that wretched town at the bottom of the mountain for three days waiting for you. I get here and there are wrecked vehicles all over the place, you're nowhere to be found, and you've moved your booze. Stupid hiding-place, anyway. I always thought it was stupid. I mean, you just don't drink enough that you need to put yourself through an obstacle course to get a reward for yourself when you're on schedule——' He stopped, his eyes roving over Jesse's shoulder. His eyes widened and his mouth fell open.

Reggie's wordless surprise lasted at least three seconds, and then his eyes narrowed with shrewdness. Cunning. He crossed the kitchen in one rolling step, shoved Jesse unceremoniously out of his way, and extended a paw to Sarah.

'Good lord,' he said with enthusiasm. 'Sahara.'

She felt herself stiffen with shock, saw the surprise and question register on Jesse's face as he looked at the man, and then at her.

'Sahara?' he asked softly.

Reggie hadn't let go of her hand. His voice was booming. He winked broadly at Jesse. 'So, this is where the lovely Sahara is. You lucky devil, Harrison! Imagine being holed up here with the world's most beautiful photographer. How the hell did you two ever meet? You move in rather different circles.'

Another shock tingled up her spine. She turned startled eyes to Jesse. Harrison?

'The whole world is looking for you, missy. I had lunch with the editor of *World Faces* just the other day. Should warn you, there's talk of broken contracts in the wind.'

Her mind was still settled firmly on 'Harrison'. Struggling to make sense out of it. She knew that it was a piece of a puzzle, that it should fit into place somewhere in her mind. But it wasn't fitting.

'Now, I know you wrote Jack a letter, but believe me, I deal with the contract end of this business, and if you promised him six photos a month, you gotta deliver.' A sly smile suddenly lit his face. 'Oh, I get it. You're going to give him Harrison, are you? Well, that'll delight Jack. I've been trying to convince Harrison for years that his ugly mug would help sell magazines—not to mention books. Had a change of heart, have you, Harrison?'

'No,' Jesse said tightly, killing fury in his eyes as he gazed at her face.

'Jesse, I haven't——'

'Jesse?' Reggie boomed. 'Oh, I get it. A pet name. Cute. Speaking of contracts, Harrison, how's *Jacoby* coming? I hope you learned to type with your teeth. Har-har! Or is that what Sahara's here for? To help you work? Har-har!'

'I'm not sure that I know why *Sahara* is here,' Jesse said tightly, his eyes never leaving her face.

'Jesse, I'm not working for *World Faces*. I'm——'

'According to Jack, you're sure as hell working for *World Faces*. Now, I know you freelance, but I'd look on it as a personal favour if Jack got the pictures of Harrison.'

It clicked in her mind. She stared at Jesse. 'You're Harrison Bond,' she stated flatly.

'As if you didn't know,' he came back quietly.

'I didn't know! And it would have saved a whole lot of heartache if you would have just said so. For heaven's sake, Jesse——'

'You can cut it out, right now, Sahara. The game's up. Should have been up a long time ago. But no, I had to believe you one last time, didn't I? I had to look at those eyes again, even though I knew better. Even though I knew they chased away my reason. Congratulations. You've got yourself one hell of a scoop now, lady. But how you'll be able to look yourself in the mirror after the way you got it——'

She picked up the nearest plate and threw it at him. 'How dare you accuse me of prostitution!' The plate shattered on the wall behind him. He didn't even blink.

'Pardon me. I could have sworn that that was what it was called when a woman trades her body——' He ducked this time as the glass whistled by his ear.

'And what's it called when a man is such a fink that he lies down beside you and you don't even know his real name? What's that called?'

A car roared to life in the background, and they both stopped and stared at each other, and then dashed for the cabin door. Reggie, a rather frightened look on his face, was putting the big car in reverse.

He unrolled his window. 'Look, Harrison, I called by at a bad time. Let me know when *Jacoby*'s done. Soon, eh? We gotta deadline.'

'Reggie, if you leave, you're fired! I mean it——'

The car revved powerfully, and backed down the gravel road at an incredible speed.

'You son of a bitch,' Jesse hissed under his breath.

Sarah glared at him. 'And that goes double for you!'

'He'll be back,' Jesse said, eyeing the road narrowly. 'He'll be back because he'll want *Jacoby*.'

'Oh?' she said sweetly. 'And pray tell, who is Jacoby, if it isn't you?'

'It is me, lady,' he said with dangerous fury. 'It's my soul. And you have scooped all of that that you are ever going to.'

'Don't make me laugh. You don't have a soul.'

'Look who's talking,' he sneered.

'I didn't know you were Harrison Bond,' she said levelly.

'Don't play me for a fool any more, *Sahara*. It's just too much of a coincidence that a photographer from a national magazine happened to find my road. A photographer who lied about her name and what she did for a living.'

'How can I convince you that you're wrong? Did you ever see me with a camera around my neck?'

'No, I didn't. Can you tell me there isn't one, in the trunk of that car? If I went and pried it open right now, what would I find?'

She blanched. It was true. He would find a camera. More than one, in fact.

He looked at her coolly, taking the look on her face as answer. He whirled from her suddenly, angrily. Stalked into the living-room. A lump formed in her throat. Her drawings had all been carefully tacked up on that bare wall. It registered that he had done this before he had come to the island, before he had ever made love with her. With an action he had made the statement that she had longed to hear in words. That she was cherished, cared about, loved, respected. He had made room for her on his living-room wall—had he really intended to make room for her in his life, as well? Was she ever going to find out now?

She somehow doubted it. He ripped one of the drawings down savagely. Shoved it under her face.

'I should have seen it, don't you think? Look at this face.'

She stared numbly down at Sahara.

'A blank canvas. Anything at all could be written on that face. I chose not to believe it. I didn't think it was you.' He laughed, a furious snort of pain, like a wounded bull. 'A wasteland. I was right, first guess.'

She turned from him so that he wouldn't see the tears running down her face. He would never believe them, anyway. 'I'll go,' she said in a strained voice. 'I'll walk out of here.'

He laughed. 'Don't bother. You can't walk down that road. We both know that. And you might misconstrue it as hate if I forced you out on to that road, to stumble, to fall, to die. Uh-uh. Hate is too close to love, Sahara. Much too close. You don't inspire anything that strong in me. Stay here. Reggie will be back. And it won't bother me. Because all I feel for you is the most colossal indifference.'

She turned and ran into the bedroom, slamming the door behind her, crying as though her heart were breaking. As though? Her heart *was* breaking.

CHAPTER NINE

'SAHARA.'

Sarah stiffened. Jesse rarely spoke to her. When he did the anger was always in his voice, sparking in his eyes. Even now, in that one word that used to be her name, she heard so much contempt that she wanted to turn and run, turn and hide. But Sahara was the one who hid. Sarah did not.

'I've asked you not to call me Sahara,' she said quietly, turning briefly to look at him from the kitchen counter where she was preparing a somewhat scanty supper.

His face looked drawn and strained these days. There were lines of weariness etched about his eyes. Still, she was just about out of sympathy for him. Weren't there limits to being stubborn? At some point didn't you have to see the truth, especially if it was practically stepping on you? Perhaps his stubborn refusal to talk about their mutual cases of assumed identities really indicated something else. Really just provided him with an excuse to get out of a relationship he couldn't handle anyway. Because he was taking his moody silences too far. She had given up hope. The only hope she harboured now was that Reggie would come back *soon* and deliver her from the agony of loving a man. Loving him enough to have forgiven him

156

almost instantly for having lied to her, for not ever having trusted her enough to tell her who he really was. And she wanted to be delivered from the agony of knowing he did not love that much. She had just had to look at Jesse and her intuition had told her that he was an honourable man. Misguided, perhaps, in keeping his identity from her, but honourable still. But that courtesy was not being returned to her. How could he be under the same roof with her, and not know? Perhaps Jesse had not seen her as clearly as she had given him credit for seeing her, after all.

'I've asked you to stop calling me Jesse, to no avail,' he pointed out.

'That's quite different.' She was not trying to be cruel. 'I can't seem to help myself. I told you once that sometimes I just find that people's names don't seem to suit them. Jesse suits you. Harrison doesn't.' It was the longest conversation they'd had in three days.

'Is that right? Pray tell me why Harrison doesn't suit me?'

He was actually encouraging a conversation? She felt a small flicker of hope within her. Surely his anger had to go away some time. Surely when it started to fade he would look at her and know, simply know to his very soul, that she could never harm him. That even if she had come here with that purpose, which she hadn't—but even if she had, that motive would have been left in the muted light of a tent on a magical island.

'Harrison Bond seems too stuffy for you. I think it conjures up an image of a British gentleman in a fedora and tweeds, smoking a pipe. Besides, it sounds like a brand of paper.'

She saw the tiniest glimmer of a smile tug at his mouth, but it was savagely doused. 'I went through the cupboards this morning. We're getting very low on food.'

She nodded. 'I know.'

'Why didn't you tell me?'

'Because you look at me as if I were a piece of garbage every time I open my mouth.'

Again something flickered in his eyes. Intense pain. Perhaps even self-censure. Again it was doused savagely.

'What could you have done anyway, Jesse? It's not as though one of us can run to the corner store.' She hesitated. 'What are we going to do?' She was aware of a strange lack of fear. Here she was facing something that resembled a *real* crisis, probably for the first time in her life, and she was completely without panic. Of course, there were still several tins of food in the cupboards, but even so, a few weeks ago even the remote possibility of running out of food would have had her wild-eyed and tearing at her hair in anticipation of the worst.

Was it because she was so emotionally deadened? Or was it because Sarah Moore was safe and strong yet in some part of her?

'We're going to have to start living off the land a bit,' Jesse decided. For the first time in days his voice was conversational, without hostility, without chill. She decided she'd be wise not to take it personally. After all, he was only dealing with the business of the day. 'We'll catch some fish. Set some snares for rabbits. There's a book on the shelf about edible plant life in the area.' He frowned. 'There's a rifle and some shells on the back porch. Left by the previous inhabitants. Unfortunately, I don't know how to use it.'

Her guard was down because of his tone, for once, was without judgement, without hostility. She smiled. 'Some outlaw you are, Jesse.'

'Don't!' he snapped.

'Don't?' she prodded quietly.

'I don't want to hear how you thought I was some notorious bandit, and that's why you felt you had licence to snoop through my things. We both know it's a lie. If you tell it often enough, you'll start to believe it.'

'Or maybe you'll start to believe it,' she guessed softly.

'Maybe,' he agreed with an angry scowl.

'Jesse——'

'Please, don't.' His voice was a whisper, tired beyond weariness, an oddly broken note in it.

She turned reluctantly back to the counter. She had nothing to offer him except the words he was determined to believe were lies.

Still, out of necessity they had to spend the morning working side by side, making snares, and then setting them around the cabin. It was the first time they had been in each other's company since Reggie's arrival and revelations. It was not comfortable. It was strained and tense, and yet she was aware that it was better than nothing. Occasionally, he'd forget to snap and crackle and just be Jesse again. It never lasted long, but it happened, and it made her attempt to understand his deep sense of betrayal. She began to realise that in the very depth of his anger, in the very fact he was having trouble letting it go, she should be able to see he really and truly cared. He would not be capable of such a strong reaction if he were as indifferent as he had tried to make her believe.

Maybe it would be all right, she decided, stealing a look at Jesse out of the corner of her eye and watching him proudly and clumsily set a snare, if Reggie held off returning for just a few more days. If he would relax like this just a little bit while he was around her, she assured herself, he would eventually be brought to the truth. That she wasn't perfect. But she wasn't the arch-villainess, either. She sighed. Full circle. He was seeing her as the wicked witch of the west again.

And maybe it just wasn't realistic to invest any more hope in his coming around. Lord, he was a stubborn man. It was going to take a long, long time before he trusted her again, saw her again in the light he had seen her in on the island. She did not know how much time they had. Reggie would be back, eventually. And there was also the possibility, with the weather being so good, that an adventurous fisherman would make his way up to this remote little lake, and rescue them. Rescue? No, if it happened too soon, it would not be a rescue. It would sound the death knell on everything they could be.

She wondered a good deal why Jesse was so sensitive to publicity, to the threat of being used. She wanted to ask him, and knew that she could not. In time, he would tell her. Maybe.

That afternoon, they set out fishing lines. To her delight—no, she thought, it was probably dismay—they got a bite almost right away.

'Sarah, you'll have to bring him in.' Jesse's eyes were fastened on the jerking rod. She supposed he didn't even realise that he had called her Sarah instead of his normal, sarcastic *Sahara*.

'Careful. Very, very smooth. Don't jerk the line, and don't let it go slack. That's the way. Did you see it? It just broke the water. OK, we're getting close now. This is where he'll get away if he's going to. He's right in front of you, Sarah. Swing the line way out over the shore. Bring him right up——'

She swung the rod, and the fish landed near Jesse. It was a big one. She felt exhilarated. She dropped the rod and ran over to the flopping fish. Laughing, tried to get the hook out of its mouth. It squirmed away.

'Careful, now. He could flop right into the water.'

Jesse came over. Between the two of them they managed to capture the slippery fish and disengage the hook from its mouth.

'Nice size,' Jesse said.

Something in his tone made her look at him. She smiled inwardly, though she wouldn't have dared to do it outwardly. Were all men like this, or just her beloved Jesse? Did they say 'nice size' in that carefully schooled and uncaring tone, when their eyes were fastened on a fish with admiration, and regret?

She looked at the fish. Gasping now, its magnificence waning with its fight.

'Oh, Jesse,' she murmured. 'I don't want to——'

His eyes met hers, and he smiled slightly. 'Neither do I,' he admitted. He took the fish back to the water, held it firmly, and swished it back and forth, letting the water enter its gills. The exhausted fish gained strength, gave a mighty twist. Jesse released it. They stood together and watched it swim away. She supposed that maybe all men did try and hide their caring for the things of the earth that they were supposed to callously enjoy hunting, but she doubted that many of them would do as Jesse had just done. Admit it, admit that killing this fish would go against his grain, admit that his hunter instinct was rather overshadowed by his human one.

'I guess we'll wait until we're really hungry before we try this again,' Jesse said, and went away quietly and began reeling in the lines.

'What if we get a rabbit?' she queried softly.

He sighed, and looked at her, a reluctant warmth in his eyes. 'Sarah, you're a real sap.'

'You, too.'

'I know. Should we go and get the snares?'

She nodded her agreement.

They collected the snares. While they were at it they collected some samples of the plant life in the area to try in a salad. They actually laughed, once or twice, at the idea of trying to eat some of the wilder-looking green things. Jesse even forgot himself, once, and started teasing her about the inhumane way in which she was slaughtering a dandelion plant.

They had one of their precious tins of soup for supper, along with a very strange, but very tasty salad.

Sarah retired to her room, feeling something changing between them, afraid to pursue it. It was when you tried to hold the butterfly in your hands that he struggled to be free. But if you waited, waited with stillness and patience and goodwill within you, then he might come and light on your shoulder.

She took out her drawing materials. Flipped through them and sighed. All she seemed capable of drawing these days was Jesse.

She thought of the way his eyes had met hers as they looked over that fish. Of the reluctant tenderness in them. She put the first bold black line on the clean white paper.

The next morning, after a skimpy breakfast, Jesse came into the bedroom while she made the bed. He unlocked the cupboard. 'I'm going to work today.'

She raised an eyebrow at him. 'How are you going to do that?'

His mouth clenched stubbornly. 'I guess I'll use the hunt and peck method with one hand. This book's been put on hold too long. I'm starting to lose it.'

'That's what you meant, a long time ago, when you said you were afraid of losing it.'

He sat down on a straight-backed chair, reached for a thick sheaf of papers. 'Yeah.' Offering nothing more.

She should have left him. But she sat down on the bed, watching him. He had already dismissed her, was already moving into a different world. This is how he handles pain, she thought perceptively. That was why he was choosing to get back to work now. So that he could enter another world, and leave this one behind. She did much the same thing with her drawing.

She sighed and stood up. 'Can I help you in any way?'

'No.'

She went into the living-room, respecting his need for privacy, and yet wanting, aching to be near to him. This was what he did. This was who he was. The man who made those beautiful words. She needed to know that man.

He must have read over what he had worked on so far, before he started. It was almost an hour before he went out and turned on the generator. It made an awful noise. Her ears had become very conditioned to silence. She put her hands over them. But Jesse didn't even glance at her as he went by her, his face already preoccupied, something wonderful in it. She guessed that the noise was a small sacrifice to make.

After a while, she could hear curses coming from the bedroom. She smiled, knowing he must be terribly frustrated with his hunt and peck system. Knowing he must be making about sixty mistakes per minute.

She went and stood in the doorway. 'Are you sure I can't help?'

'Sure, Sahara,' he snapped. 'And then you can give *World Faces* a real scoop. Tell them all about *Jacoby James*, maybe give them a chapter or two.'

She sighed, turned away, felt the tears slither down her cheeks. At least she knew, now, who Jacoby James was. Of course, she had suspected for some time that it was a book. In a way, she didn't think it was such a terrible lie, that he had taken the name of the star of his next book. While he was writing, he probably became very much a part of the person he was writing about. So much a part that she was willing to bet that that was why he came here when he was finally ready to write. To find himself again, to separate himself from the characters that his book-jackets said he spent up to a year living with before he even attempted to write their stories.

Jesse looked furious and frustrated by lunchtime. He was exuding an enormous energy that she suspected didn't match his ability to get the words down on to paper.

'How's it going?' she asked tentatively.

He gave her a black look. 'I can't do it. My hand can't keep up with the flow of words. It's just making me angry. My mind is in one place, being held back by a technical limitation.' He swore.

'I can type, Jesse.'

His eyes widened, and then narrowed. '*You* can type?'

She nodded, smiled ruefully. 'I haven't for years. I suppose I'd be pretty rusty. But it's probably like riding a bicycle.' Her rueful smile deepened. 'Which is something I've never done.'

'You've never ridden a bicycle?' he asked with astonishment.

She shook her head. 'I wasn't allowed to do anything that might put a scrape or a scratch on my knees or elbows or face. My mother didn't even want me to take typing. She thought I might break a fingernail—I have very photogenic hands. I was getting lots of lotion and fingernail work at that time. Occasionally, I managed to stand up to my mother. Very occasionally.'

'Get up,' he said roughly.

'What?'

'Don't get the wrong idea, Sarah Moore. I will never forgive you for coming here under false pretences. I will never expose any more of myself to you than I have to. But if you're twisted and unfeeling, I'm beginning to wonder how much of it is your fault. Never ridden a bicycle because somebody thought you might get a scratch?'

He was furious. She stared at him with astonishment.

'Get up,' he said again roughly.

She got up and followed him as he grabbed his crutch and went out of the cabin. He walked through the hole in the shed that the truck had left. She went in behind him, squinting.

'There it is,' he said.

'What?'

'The bicycle. Get it.'

He turned and walked back into the sunshine. She hauled out the bicycle.

He inspected it. 'The kids who were here before left it. I can see why. Still, it'll run.'

'The tyres are flat,' she pointed out, watching him with amusement.

He stamped back into the shed, came out with a bicycle pump. One-armed, he managed to get the tyres inflated.

'Get on,' he snapped.

'Jesse——'

He took a menacing step towards her. She threw a long leg over the bicycle. Stood there with it between her legs, not altogether certain what to do.

'Get up on the seat, and start pedalling.'

She rolled her eyes, but did as she was told. The bicycle wobbled, and she fell over. She giggled.

'Do it again.'

She did it again and again, her wobbly little trips lasting longer and longer. She was laughing. She was laughing so hard she could barely stay on the bike. It seemed quite hopeless, actually, but then suddenly something clicked. She wasn't sure what. Suddenly she was actually riding the bike, pedalling furiously down the gravel path that led out towards the main road. She didn't know how to stop and didn't want to. She went out on to the main road, pedalling breathlessly, feeling the wind in her face, feeling the laughter rippling out of her. And behind her she could hear Jesse, laughing, sharing her joy. She looked over her shoulder, fell off the bike, and lay there, content, laughing. She got back on the bike and rode back to Jesse.

He stared at her face for a long time. Then, wordlessly, his face closed, he turned and clumped away.

He was silent and uncommunicative that night. She read one of his books. It was the next best thing to having him. There was so much of Jesse in these books. The vulnerability underneath the cool exterior, the softness, the sensitivity underneath the hardness. She wondered sadly if this was all she would have of him. His books, to keep her company on long winter nights. The drawings she had done of him. The picture she would always hold of him in her mind.

She thought of him insisting that she ride that bike. He was trying so hard not to care, and caring anyway. How strong was Jesse? How long could he fight himself? How long could he ignore the intuitive voice that was trying to break through his wall of anger, trying to tell him that he was wrong about her? Dreadfully wrong. He was very strong, and very stubborn. She supposed that it could go on forever. Forever. A word that seemed rather bleak without Jesse in the picture.

Bleak, yes; hopeless, no. Because she had Sarah now. And Sarah was never going away again. And Sarah was going to make a life for herself. It would involve drawing. She was eager to move into painting. It was probably going to involve a place of her own, in mountains like these ones, at a lake like this one.

'You really can type?' Jesse asked her the next morning.

Her heart caught in her throat. 'Really,' she confirmed.

'Fine, let's get to work.'

She studied him. Was he trusting her? She didn't think so. She thought his thirst to get back to work was making him stoop to any level. His need to outrun his pain was making him extend a most reluctant trust to her.

He explained Jacoby to her. It was the story of an old rancher who lived by himself and ran a small ranch in an isolated part of Montana. Jesse had spent a year with him. Getting to know him, researching, living in his pocket.

He settled on his bed. Closed his eyes. Began to talk, very slowly.

She struggled to keep up. Her typing was very rusty, and he tended to get caught up in his words and start to race on. But by mid-afternoon they had hit a rhythm. Her hands were screaming their protest, but her mind was energetic and alert. The story was incredibly beautiful and compelling, and it was Jesse who had to suggest that they take a break.

By the end of the day, they were a team. Jesse was in good spirits, his barriers were down. He looked over the typed pages with a deep satisfaction.

'Thank you,' he said to her.

'You're welcome. I enjoyed it. It's a beautiful story, Jesse.'

Something in his face closed. 'Is that what you'll tell *World Faces*?'

'You are a stupid, stupid man!'

'Why is that?' His voice was silky and unperturbed.

'Do you really think I'd sit here and work myself to exhaustion for a scoop for *World Faces*? What on earth would my motive be, Jesse?'

'How on earth would I know?' he said cynically.

'Oh, from the expert on human motivations. Well, tell me, Mr Expert. What would motivate me? Money? Glory?'

'I suppose both of those,' he said.

The anger left her voice. It became soft and sad. 'I've had them both, Jesse. I've had more glory, more glamour, more attention, than the Queen. And I've made more money than I can spend in my lifetime. Neither of those things means anything.'

'So you tell me then—what was your motivation?'

'You stupid, stupid man,' she repeated, but this time with sadness that cut through to her soul, rather than anger. 'If I have to tell you, it's worth nothing. Nothing.' She turned and walked away, stopped and gazed back at him. 'What was your motivation for teaching me to ride a bicycle?'

'I have no idea,' he said coldly. 'I guess it seemed like a good way to kill time.'

'You're a liar, Harrison Bond.'

She went out into the cool night, gazed at the lake for a long time. He did it for love. Just as she did it for love. But could love grow once it had been exposed to the light of betrayal, of mistrust? Perhaps, but perhaps it only grew twisted.

Her eyes caught on the bicycle, leaning innocently against the house. She didn't know if she could walk out of here. She was a different person from the one who had arrived here so adamant about her limitations. She did know that almost from the very beginning she had stayed, not because she felt she had to, but because she had wanted to. No, she still wasn't sure about the walk. But she did know that she no longer wanted to stay here, and that, as an adult woman, she did not have to do things she did not want to do. She had to make choices rather than allow herself to be trapped by, made a victim of, circumstance. She could ride a bicycle. She knew she could do that. Her resolve firmed. First thing in the morning, she would leave Harrison Bond far behind her.

No, not Harrison Bond. Jesse. Her beloved Jesse.

She got up very early. Stopped in the living-room and looked very quietly down at his sleeping face. Lord, he was a handsome man. Lord, she would miss him. He looked different asleep. More open, more vulnerable, younger.

She couldn't resist. Tenderly and ever so lightly she ran her fingers through his hair, and then swiftly dropped a feather-light kiss upon his cheek.

He opened his eyes, briefly. 'Argh,' he said. All his anger, all his sense of betrayal, in that one growled phrase. Once he had found her homely outwardly. Now he found her ugly within, could not bear the feel of her lips on his cheek.

And she could not bear that any longer. 'Goodbye, Jesse.'

She went and got on the bicycle. She stopped once, just as the road twisted, and glanced back at the cabin. Her heart ached within her, feeling as though it would burst.

Jesse stumbled out on to the porch and stared at her, the lines of his face proud, fierce, unyielding.

Still, she waited momentarily. Shut her eyes. Hoped and prayed he would call her name, ask her not to leave him.

He stood in stony silence. She focused on the road in front of her. Pedalled out of view.

CHAPTER TEN

SARAH gazed dully out of the window of the tow-truck. They were on the road now, the road that led to Jesse's cabin. She had sworn, after that long, tortured bicycle ride, that she would never come on this road again. Had that only been a week ago? It seemed like a lifetime.

She remembered her first time on this road. How dark it had been. How ominous. How she had believed with her whole heart and soul that she was headed into outlaw country. And so she had been. The outlaw country of her own heart.

'I can't believe you couldn't find my car,' she said to the burly man driving the truck. 'You must know this area like the back of your hand.'

He shrugged, and slid her a look she was too heartsore to try and interpret. They came to the car and he pulled over, bashed his horn with his elbow getting out of the truck. She nearly jumped out of her skin. She glanced warily at the road, and then glared at him. He treated her to a gap-toothed grin. Strolled leisurely around her car. Scratched his head.

'Would you get on with it?' she hissed.

He looked at her with wounded dignity. 'Thar's more to this job than ya might 'magine, ma'am.'

The sound of a car starting broke the silence of the lake country. Her nerves tingled, and she looked around for a place to hide. No, that was being silly. She pulled herself up to her full height, and eyed the road with what she could only hope was all the cool hauteur of years in the modelling business.

Reggie's big car came around the curve in the road. She felt her whole body go weak with relief—and maybe disappointment. Oh, to gaze just once more into the crystal-clear green of those eyes.

The car stopped. A tinted window purred down. She gazed once more into the crystal-clear of those green eyes.

'Hi,' he said softly.

She nodded curtly at him.

'Thanks for sending help. I'm not sure I deserved it.'

'Me neither,' she said coldly.

'You did a good job on my arm. The doctors were impressed.'

'Great.' Inwardly she willed him to go away. She did not want to stand here making small talk, did not want to hear his carefully phrased words of gratitude before he said goodbye for good.

'Could we talk?' he said softly.

'I don't think so.'

'Looks as if I just wasted a hundred bucks then,' he said sadly, but faint amusement was glowing in his eyes.

'Pardon?'

'That's what it cost to get Henry to drag you up here.'

She stared at the tow-truck driver. He caught her look. Winked. She turned back to Jesse. 'You son of a——'

'That's the Sarah I know and love,' he said softly.

Her whole spine stiffened. Love? But such a casual turn of phrase. She would be a fool to read anything into it.

'What do you say, Sarah? Could I have about a hundred dollars' worth of your time?'

She looked at him haughtily. 'That's about one minute of my time.'

He nodded. 'OK. I'll take it. Get in.'

She hesitated, and then stalked over to the passenger side, got in, sat with her arms folded across her chest staring straight ahead. Jesse exchanged a few low words with the tow-truck driver, then put the car in gear.

'One minute doesn't give you time to go very far,' she reminded him acidly.

'Maybe I could have ten minutes? On credit?'

'Fine. Take as long as you want. I'll send you a bill.' She slid him a look, and her heart squeezed painfully. He looked haggard. Worn out. His face was dark with stubble from his beard. There were shadows under his eyes.

He turned the car around and drove to the end of the road, a point slightly past the cabin that overlooked the whole lake. Her eyes caught on the little island. She wondered if the deer was still there. She wondered if the magic was still there. Her hauteur collapsed. She began to cry.

'Don't,' he whispered. His arm came around her, and he pulled her into the wall of his chest. 'Please don't cry, Sarah.'

'I happen to have a lot to cry about,' she sniffed, with a poor attempt at dignity.

'You do,' he agreed. 'First and foremost, you fell in love with a man like me.'

'Don't flatter yourself!' she snapped, pulling away from him.

'Sarah, you left your drawings here.'

'Yes, I know. I'd like them back, please.'

'There are so many of me,' he said thoughtfully.

'You were a readily available subject,' she said, having regained her composure. 'I was just making up for the fact that I didn't have a camera. I intend to sell those drawings to *World Faces*.'

'Sarah, what if I tell you I was ten kinds of a fool?'

'I'd agree,' she said flatly.

'Sarah, it's in them. In the drawings.'

'What is?'

'How much you love me.'

'Humph. What if I told you I was ten kinds of a fool?'

'I'd believe you. You picked a hard man to love.' He gazed out of the window. 'Nobody ever loved *me*, Sarah. Nobody ever saw Jesse before. Not as you did. Oh, plenty of women have loved Harrison Bond.' He sighed. 'All those photos? Thanks to a long-ago publicity prank of Reggie's, I became the literary world's answer to Robert Redford. I mean, it's a joke. It's a bad joke that just won't go away.

I was not cut out to be a sex symbol. And yet all these women keep on accosting me in public places and writing me letters. They write how much they love me. Some of them want to meet me, some of them want to marry me, sight unseen. Occasionally someone mentions my writing.' His mouth twisted wryly. 'It's so ridiculous it's hard to believe. But, you know, there's such a lonely desperation in some of those letters that I can never quite bring myself to throw the pictures away. I mean, somebody sends you a picture, and they're trying to say, this is who I am, they're asking you to see through the surface and look at their souls. I look at those pictures and I see vulnerable, lonely people. They buy my books. I owe them something. I can never throw the pictures in the garbage.

'When this all started it was a real shock to me. I was a shy kid, a shy young man. A bookworm. Women never gave me a second look.'

'Are you kidding, Jesse?' she said with astonishment.

He smiled, shook his head. 'I was really skinny, and had terrible acne until I was in my early twenties. I started to fill out and lost the acne at about the same time my first book hit the stands. And suddenly this shy young man was being thronged with adoration. Drowning in it. I married the woman who seemed to adore me the most. A gorgeous, petite little blonde named Karen. And found out she didn't love me at all. She loved the name, the status, the fame. She didn't even know me, let alone love me. Two-way street, though. I didn't know her, either.

'I'm very private, and she couldn't understand that. She wanted me to milk the fame for all it was worth. Accept the invitations to the famous people's parties, do all the interviews and the talk shows. So that she could hold up magazine articles to her friends and say, "This is who my husband is" when she really didn't have a clue, and didn't care, who her husband really was.

'My aversion for publicity just grew under her pressure. The marriage, if it could even be called that, lasted less than two years. My aversion to publicity is all that's left from it. And that very aversion seems to make me a hotter item than ever. I'd be a real coup for some fledgling reporter to bring in. And you wouldn't believe the lengths some of these people have gone to, to get a picture I don't want taken, to get an interview I don't want to give.

'Then I met a woman, Inge, while I was on holiday in Switzerland. I really, really liked her. We explored the Alps together. We had an affair. She turned out to be a reporter for a gossip magazine. The most private part of my life was put on display for a drooling public. I've rarely felt killing anger, but I did then. There were a few more similiar, though not as devastating occurrences, and I started to take steps that would almost be called paranoid to protect myself against people who would use me. I thought I'd become a very good judge of people. Could tell in a glance what they wanted, who they were.

'And then you came along. I could never tell with you, Sarah. I could never tell who you were or what you wanted. Until we spent that time on the island. And then I thought I knew.'

'Oh, Jesse,' she whispered, 'no wonder you couldn't tell who I was or what I wanted. I never knew myself. Until that time we spent on the island.'

'Tell me now, Sarah, tell me who you are and what you want.'

She nodded. 'All right. But first I'll tell you who I'm not, and what I don't want. I'm not Sahara. My mother was an extraordinarily beautiful woman. Her dream was to be a top-flight model, an actress. An accidental pregnancy and an early marriage put an end to that dream. Sort of. But not really, because she just continued her dream through me. Started pouring all her raw ambition into me when I was a baby. I was eight months old when she landed my first ad campaign. It was for Tot-a-bot Baby Food. I was entered in every beautiful baby contest, as I got older I was entered in every talent contest—I twirled a baton, and tap-danced—every beauty contest. I made the rounds of all the ad agencies. I was Little Miss Grape Juice one year. Little Miss California Raisin the next. It went on and on. When I was fourteen my mother entered me in a search-for-talent contest sponsored by a top modelling agency. I think there were ten thousand hopeful girls in that contest. I won.

'I was the perfect model. Because I could be anything anybody wanted me to be. You want sweetness? You've got it. You want smouldering passion? I can do that. You want sultry or sulky or fresh or athletic? I can be anything. I could be anything, because I was a blank piece of paper waiting to be written on. I learned very early how to get approval. To gauge what other people, especially my mother, wanted, and be just that.

'And, underneath, I was amazed. I was none of the things I was so good at pretending I was when I posed for the camera. I kept expecting someone to see it, to love the real person underneath. Nobody ever did. They saw the beauty and the glamour, and that was all.

'Models don't last long. Cameras are cruel. They pick up lines and shadows that the human eye can barely see. Very young faces photograph the best. The skin has a quality of unbelievable freshness. Unlined. Translucent. By the time I was eighteen, my mother was starting to look at me critically. Was moaning that I'd be doing catalogue ads before long. She wanted me to get into acting. To use the fame Sahara had built as a model to explode into a brand-new career. I went along, until I was told my voice wasn't right. No problem, said Mama Bear, we'll change the voice.

'And I finally had the maturity, or the survival instinct, to say no. I became a photographer instead. And I loved it. Boy, I was the one in control now. I was the one telling people how to look and pose. I had the top magazines in the world begging me to do photography for them. Movie stars and celebrities calling to see if I'd like to do their picture.

'You won't believe how naïve I was. I never even noticed that when I had a picture published, a picture of me taking the picture was almost always included. A picture with a caption that read something like "world-famous model, now turned photographer, Sahara, blah, blah, blah..."'

'Oh, Sarah,' Jesse said softly, gently.

'I was still being used, and I was too damned stupid to realise it. Somebody had to tell me. Nelson told me.'

'Nelson?' Jesse stiffened.

She laughed tremulously. 'The one person I thought loved me, Jesse—I thought he really loved me. I asked him to marry me. The man is sixty years old. A very debonair, young sixty, but sixty. I didn't love him. I realise that now. I thought he was safe. I thought he, of all of them, just enjoyed me. Didn't want anything from me, didn't want to be able to list Sahara as one of his conquests.

'In the end he had to tell me he was using me. I couldn't see it for myself. He had to tell me it was his way of holding on to the limelight long past the time he should have. He liked being seen with this young, successful model. Liked having his picture published in the society page, in the glossy magazines. But he didn't like me.

'He laid it on the line that night. For a long time I believed he was just being cruel. He let me know how everybody, including Mother, used me. He let me know I wasn't a photographer. He said people only bought my pictures because I was famous. That I was a dreadful photographer.

'I set out to prove him wrong. I sent out piles of my photographs to magazines and papers, using a pseudonym. I'd show Nelson.

'Nobody wanted those pictures. Not a single person. Some of them wrote back quite caustic notes that they did not accept such amateur work.

'And so instead of having a good hard look at myself I came out here, looking for my father. I wasn't a model. I wasn't a photographer. I wasn't anything at all. My dad was going to be able to tell me who I was. Maybe I was hoping I could be Daddy's little girl, since I was nothing else. Maybe that was what I was doing with Nelson all those years. Looking for a daddy, to love me unconditionally, wanting it so badly I wouldn't have believed the truth if it hit me over the head.

'And then I met you, Jesse. And you didn't see any of the things the rest of the world had always seen. You saw me, me struggling and trying to become. You saw me being born, and you saw Sahara dying. No wonder you couldn't understand, couldn't be sure who I was or what I wanted.'

'Who are you, Sarah? And what do you want?' he asked softly.

She turned and met his eyes for the first time. 'I'm Sarah Moore. I'm an artist. I'm a strong and resilient and stubborn and temperamental human being. I'm good and I'm bad. I'm a child and a woman. I'm becoming me. I want to work at that for the rest of my life. It's the only thing that's ever felt real, that's ever felt good. I feel alive, Jesse, and I plan to stay that way.'

'And is there room in all this for an outlaw?' he asked softly.

'Yes,' she whispered. 'There's room for an outlaw. Room for two outlaws. You and me.'

He reached over, his lips found hers. They kissed endlessly, passion and acceptance and love all riding within them on those prancing, dancing horses that were their spirits.

She looked longingly at the cabin. 'Damn. I suppose Reggie is here.'

'Uh-uh,' he murmured into her hair. 'I made him leave the car, since I won't be able to drive a standard for a while.'

'So we're not marooned?' she asked, her brow furrowing into a frown.

'No.'

They drove back to the cabin. Jesse got out and held open the door for her. She slid past the instrument panel, and hesitated.

'What are you doing?' Jesse asked, a certain hoarse urgency in his voice.

'Nothing. My skirt seems to be caught . . . there.' And she took his extended hand, felt the eagerness and need and love in the way his fingers closed around hers.

'What about the tow-truck driver?' she asked as they went into the cabin.

'He won't be disturbing us. When you were coming around to get in the car, I told him there was an extra hundred in it for him if he just hooked your car up, dragged it away, and never came back.'

'You're pretty loose with your money, Jesse. By the way, you owe me about ten thousand dollars.'

'Take it out in trade?' he asked, nibbling her neck and pushing her backwards on to the bed that had been hers and would now be theirs.

'All right,' she agreed huskily when his lips dropped lower. At the touch of his lips, she realised that a part of her had died when she had ridden down the mountain. No, not died. Gone to sleep, waiting within her for the kiss of her prince that it might blossom again.

And it did blossom; she opened with swift and incredible drama, like the opening of a flower shown through time-lapse photography. There was no hesitation left in her, no overshadowing of doubt, no shyness, no holding back. This man belonged to her heart. He was hers to taste, and to touch, to worship with her lips and her tongue and her caressing fingertips.

And she was his. There was an unspoken promise in their lovemaking that had not been there before. It whispered of tomorrow. In a language without words, it vowed to cherish this blessed gift of love that had been bestowed on them. Bestowed on them by something bigger than them, something that had put a wrong turn on the right map all those weeks ago...

It was later, much, much later, when she turned to him and laid her head against his chest. 'It's Jones Lake,' she said suddenly.

Jesse's hand tangled in her hair. His lips found the hollow of her shoulder. 'What?' he asked, slightly baffled, mostly uncaring.

'My father lives at Jones Lake.'

'Never heard of it,' he murmured, and his lips moved from the hollow of her shoulder to the dip of throat.

'It's eighty miles west of here...I took a wrong— Jesse, are you listening to me?'

'Hmmm, eighty miles west...' his voice was lost somewhere in the gentle swell of her breast.

'I'd like to see him...some time.'

'Me, too.' His lips stopped their exploring, and he took her hand and placed it to his cheek. His eyes roved over her face with tender and tamed wonder. 'Yes, I'd very much like to meet him. An old-fashioned part of me wants to say "Sir, I'd like to ask your permission to have your daughter's hand in marriage." Does that sound unbearably corny?'

'Unbearably,' she agreed, but a brilliant smile had lit her lips and brilliant tears coursed down her cheeks.

'Maybe we should drive down there tomorrow.'

'Oh. I don't think we'll be driving anywhere tomorrow. I've waited many years to meet my father. A few more weeks won't hurt.'

'Weeks?'

'Perhaps we could have our honeymoon before the wedding, since we're kind of stuck here anyway.'

'Kind of stuck here?'

'I turned on the car lights, Jesse.'

He laughed throatily. 'Should have thought of it myself.' His eyes lit on her lips and the laughter died between them.

'Wait,' she said suddenly, pushing him away. 'There is one more thing I need to know before I commit my life to you,' she informed him sternly.

'What's that?'

'Who in the world is Tony Lama?'

'Who?'

'Tony Lama. That first morning, I woke up and you were muttering about Tony Lama. I thought the name sounded very Italian. I thought you must have a Mafia connection.'

Jesse threw back his head and laughed. 'Good lord, Sarah, life is never going to have a dull moment around you, is it? Your mind works in a way nobody else's does. I'll be unravelling you endlessly. I can't wait for every day to bring me some delightful new side of that quirky mind.'

'Are you avoiding the question?'

'No, ma'am. Tony Lama makes boots.'

'Makes boots?' Her eyes widened. 'Do you mean makes books?'

'No.'

'A bootlegger?'

'He makes boots, Sarah. The best Western boots in the world. Just like the one you sawed off my leg. Come to think of it, you owe me——'

'Take it out in trade?' she whispered into his ear.

'What are we going to do when all the scores are evened?' he teased with mock trepidation.

'We'll think of something,' she assured him, and her lips caught his.

Later, much later, she lay tangled in the circle of his arms. Her eyes were closed, she felt utterly relaxed, and her mind drifted.

He stood there, the blazing sun setting at his back. Behind him a spirited stallion stamped impatiently. The man was a picture of strength, of cool invulnerability. And yet there was something else in him, too. A loneliness, an aching need that hid in the furthest reaches of those dancing green eyes.

She had the eyes to see that which only a very few, a trusted few, would ever see about this man. She went to him. Traced the proud lines of his face with her fingertips, and looked deep into his outlaw eyes.

And saw a man. Saw a man whose wariness melted as he drank in her upturned face, whose hardness fell away under her tender touch.

He scooped her up in his powerful arms, stilled her laughter with feather-light kisses of passion and of promise. He tossed her up into the saddle of the waiting horse, swung on behind her, and then spurred the magnificent animal towards the setting sun.

And towards the final frontier. Outlaw

country. That uncharted territory where all the tender secrets of human hearts lay waiting to be discovered.

HARLEQUIN PROUDLY PRESENTS A
DAZZLING CONCEPT IN ROMANCE FICTION

One small town,
twelve terrific love stories.

TYLER—GREAT READING... GREAT SAVINGS...
AND A FABULOUS FREE GIFT

Each book set in Tyler is a self-contained love story;
together, the twelve novels stitch the fabric of
the community.

By collecting proofs-of-purchase found in each Tyler
book, you can receive a fabulous gift, ABSOLUTELY
FREE! And use our special Tyler coupons to save on
your next Tyler book purchase.

Join us for the third Tyler book, WISCONSIN
WEDDING by Carla Neggers, available in May.

If you missed *Whirlwind* (March) or *Bright Hopes* (April) and would like to order them, send
your name, address, zip or postal code, along with a check or money order for $3.99 (please
do not send cash), plus 75¢ postage and handling ($1.00 in Canada) for each book ordered,
payable to Harlequin Reader Service to:

In the U.S.

3010 Walden Avenue
P.O. Box 1325
Buffalo, NY 14269-1325

In Canada

P.O. Box 609
Fort Erie, Ontario
L2A 5X3

Please specify book title(s) with your order.

Canadian residents add applicable federal and provincial taxes.

TYLER-3

Following the success of WITH THIS RING,
Harlequin cordially invites you to enjoy the
romance of the wedding season with

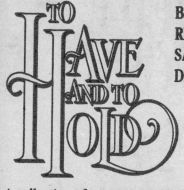

**BARBARA BRETTON
RITA CLAY ESTRADA
SANDRA JAMES
DEBBIE MACOMBER**

A collection of romantic stories that celebrate the joy,
excitement, and mishaps of planning that special day
by these four award-winning Harlequin authors.

**Available in April at your favorite Harlequin
retail outlets.**

℮ *Harlequin* ®

JANELLE TAYLOR

Valley of Fire

HARLEQUIN IS PROUD TO PRESENT *VALLEY OF FIRE* BY JANELLE TAYLOR—AUTHOR OF TWENTY-TWO BOOKS, INCLUDING SIX *NEW YORK TIMES* BESTSELLERS

VALLEY OF FIRE—the warm and passionate story of Kathy Alexander, a famous romance author, and Steven Winngate, entrepreneur and owner of the magazine that intended to expose the real Kathy "Brandy" Alexander to her fans.

Don't miss VALLEY OF FIRE, available in May.